Melanie

❧ BOOK 4 ❧

Orphan Train Series

Wendy May Andrews

ᘒ

Sparrow Ink
www.sparrowink.com

Stay in touch with Wendy May Andrews
and forthcoming publishing news.

Sign up for her biweekly newsletter

Two challenged hearts. One true love?

The death of her mother left ten-year-old Melanie Jones with too many responsibilities. Raising her younger siblings under the weight of her father's unkind words filled her with insecurities. Despite those early years, she's determined to make a new life for herself. Moving far away from home, she boards a train to escort the latest load of orphans to Missouri.

Abandoned by his wife then widowed, Cole Miller is forced to raise his daughter on his own. Though his sister is supposed to help, she's more liability than asset. When a beautiful newcomer arrives in town, her doubts and insecurities leave Cole uninterested. He's had his fill of women like his wife and sister.

When Melanie steps in to help Cole with his daughter, he's able to see beyond her timidity and discover her beautiful and gracious soul. Will his discovery be enough for him to let go of his own uncertainties? Is Melanie ready for a family of her own?

Dedication

To Mum & Dad who gave me the foundation upon which I stand.

This heroine holds a special place in my heart. Melanie struggles with her insecurities and would much rather stay home than face people. This book is for all those who feel alone as they face their challenges.

And for my own home hero who makes sure I'm not alone as I face mine.

Acknowledgements

As always, my awesome beta readers:
Marlene, Suzanne, Monique, and Alfred, helped me
immeasurably. Then, my lovely editor, Julie Spencer, took it all
and made it shine. All remaining messiness is my own efforts.
Also, special thanks go to Les at "GermanCreative" for all the
gorgeous covers in this series.

Chapter One

Bucklin, Missouri - Early summer 1854

Melanie stared at the handsome man. She hadn't expected him to be so good looking. She quickly realized that was a ridiculous thought. Why wouldn't he be? She hadn't actually given the man's appearance any thought, so she shouldn't be quite this surprised by his flawless face and clear blue gaze. In fact, given how pretty little Mary was, it should have been expected. But nonetheless, she felt tongue tied and gauche and dearly wished she had not made arrangements for Annie to stay over at her friend's house.

"You must be Annie," the man said in a smooth baritone that did funny things to Melanie's stomach while Annie nodded and grinned. "And you must be Mrs. Carter," he continued, looking at Melanie.

Her nervous giggle embarrassed her as she shook her head. "No, I'm sorry for the confusion, I'm Melanie Jones, Mrs. Carter's housemate. Mrs. Carter being unavailable today is part of why I agreed to Annie coming to stay over when your wife asked this morning."

Mr. Miller's smile should be outlawed, Melanie thought as she blinked, hoping she didn't look like a dull-witted bovine as she did so. *But why is he grinning like that?* The thought flitted through her head just as he chuckled.

"Leandra's not my wife. She's my sister. She came out here to help me and Mary when my wife died."

"Oh no, I'm so sorry for your loss."

The handsome man lifted a shoulder in a half shrug. She could relate to the feeling. Really, what is there that can be said? Losing someone in death is the most permanent form of tragedy. And anyone saying sorry about it is kind but rather useless. There's nothing that can be done.

"It's good that you have had your sister to help you out," she added.

The look he gave her led her to believe that maybe his sister hadn't been such a help after all. *This is why I don't deal with people*, Melanie thought with a twinge of anguish. She hated the awkwardness she always felt when she was with other people. Her insecurities made interacting with strangers nearly debilitating. Once again, she was grateful for her business partner's willingness to deal with their customers.

Mary's father interrupted the flow of her disquieting thoughts. "Is there anything we need to know about Annie?"

Melanie's heart sank. She knew so little about the poor child. "She's a delight and doesn't make a fuss about much of anything, so you should be fine."

"Has she slept over at someone's house before?" Mr. Miller pressed.

"In a manner of speaking," Melanie answered, wondering if she ought to air Katie and Annie's business. With a mental shrug, she figured it wasn't all that private a matter. "Annie has just recently joined our household. Mrs. Carter adopted Annie. The sweet child has seemed to take it all in her stride so well that I suspect you won't have any problems with her."

Mr. Miller looked at her with curiosity clearly evident on his face, and Melanie fought the urge to squirm. "Would you like to come in for a cup of tea or coffee while we see if the girls settle in all right?"

Melanie quite strongly wanted to decline the invitation but when she glanced down at Annie, seeing the hesitation on the child's face, she realized she ought to do what she could to make sure Annie was comfortable. Melanie would have to set aside her own discomfort this time. Negative thoughts crowded around in her head as she struggled with regrets that she hadn't insisted Katie not adopt the little girl. But Melanie did her best to reject the negativity. Annie was a delightful child, and Melanie couldn't begrudge either her or Katie their newfound familial happiness.

Pasting what she hoped wasn't an overtly fake-looking smile onto her face, Melanie nodded and accepted the man's offer. "I suppose that might be wise."

When one side of the man's handsome face lifted into a lopsided grin, Melanie questioned her own words. No, it was not wise to spend any amount of time around him. She was sure to be tongue tied and awkward. She wished she could fall into a conveniently opened hole in the floor. But those things never happened, no matter how hard one wished for them. She swallowed her nerves as best she could and followed the two little girls and the large man into the house.

Glancing around, Melanie was surprised to see very little evidence of a woman's touch in the clean but sparse house. It would seem Leandra was not leaving her mark on her brother's home. To her chagrin, Mr. Miller must have read the curiosity on her face.

"My sister hasn't been enjoying her time her in Missouri. She is determined to return East as soon as possible, even though she has been here for almost two years now. I think now that Mary is in school, we'll be able to manage without her. I should really put Leandra on the next train headed east, but I find myself struggling with nerves."

Melanie was shocked to hear a man admitting to such a feeling. "What are you nervous about?" She colored slightly at the emphasis on "you" as it revealed her own issues, but she brazened it out and waited for his reply.

He shrugged and offered her another lopsided grin. "What do I know about little girls? Or big girls for that matter. I hate keeping Leandra here when I know she's hating it, but I hate even more the thought of Mary not having the best care."

Melanie glanced around to make sure the girls were out of earshot but also ensured to keep her voice low as she answered him. "Children are remarkably perceptive and are affected by how they think the adults around them are feeling. I have had a great deal of experience with children. In my opinion, Mary will thrive if she knows you care about her and are doing your best. I don't know her well, but she seems like a bright, happy child. I don't think you have to worry overly." She paused for a moment before adding, "It speaks well of you that you have even given the matter some thought. Most men wouldn't."

Mr. Miller offered her a quizzical glance but didn't comment, merely busying himself getting the water on to boil. Melanie tried to keep her focus away from him, but she couldn't help being fascinated by the sight of a man moving around a kitchen as though he knew what he was doing there. His large hands managed to handle the kettle dexterously and scoop the roughly ground coffee without spilling. When it came time to set out the dainty cups, Melanie had to bite her lip to prevent a grin from spreading across her face. She wondered why he had such delicate things. She was embarrassed to realize her thoughts must have written themselves on her face when he looked at her with his eyebrows quirked quizzically. The color rose in his cheeks, but his gaze never wavered. He lifted his shoulder.

"My daughter loves to play tea parties, and a good tin cup just won't do for her. She has convinced me that a well-equipped kitchen is fully stocked with teacups and nothing less should ever be offered to a proper lady."

Melanie allowed her grin to spread. "Well, I'm honored that you think me a proper lady, in that case."

His answering grin made her nerves flutter, but she managed not to cower away, grateful beyond words when he didn't seem to notice, merely turning back to competently set out the coffee that was now ready. He placed a plate of cookies on the table between them as he sat down across from her.

Chapter Two

Cole watched in amazement as his guest nibbled on a cookie. It was better than when she had been nibbling on her lip. He had to work hard not to stare. She was obviously high strung. After the trouble he had been dealing with because of his sister, he should be completely unaffected by her nervous fidgets. But instead, he had to fight an overwhelming impulse to draw her into his arms and comfort her. It was the strangest sensation. The only other person he felt so protective towards was Mary. But the sensations he was feeling towards Miss Jones were most certainly not of the paternal type. It was definitely time for some conversation to divert the mood in the room.

"How are you enjoying life in Bucklin thus far, Miss Jones?"

He tried not to be charmed by the blush that colored her cheekbones as her eyes bounced around the room. Apparently, conversation wasn't going to help the situation. Cole stifled a sigh. He was glad he managed to retain a modicum of patience. It was soon rewarded.

With a deep breath that seemed to go all the way to her toes and an effort that appeared truly valiant, she brought her gaze to meet his and finally answered his question.

"I actually quite like it, Mr. Miller. Anyone I've met has been remarkably kind. Katie, I mean Mrs. Carter, and I cannot get over how clean everything is. We had rather expected it to be dry and dusty, but it's not. It's much more green than I thought it would be. And the air and water are so clean. We remark on it nearly every day."

Cole watched in fascination as she became more and more animated as she talked, as though she were able to forget whatever caused her fears as she warmed to her subject.

"Did you not have clean air and water where you come from?" He knew she was from New York but didn't think that great city was so very dirty.

"Have you ever been to New York, Mr. Miller?"

"I'm originally from Boston, myself. I had visited, of course, in the course of business, but I haven't spent much time there. None at all in the past seven years, of course. Since we moved out here, I have had absolutely no desire to return East."

"I can fully understand such a sentiment." She nodded and smiled, seemingly a completely different person than the one who had arrived on his doorstep half an hour ago. Cole wanted to extend their time together.

"You aren't feeling homesick?" He couldn't help the surprise from sounding in his voice.

Her cheeks turned pink and Cole held his breath, hoping she didn't turn into the nervous wraith she had been earlier. Her shoulders lifted in a small shrug.

"There isn't much home to be sick for, I'm afraid. New York doesn't hold anything for me anymore. Everything here is so lovely. I can see this being my home forever."

Cole hesitated to ask, certain it would put her walls back up, but he couldn't just leave it.

"Are you one of the orphans, too?"

She offered him a half-hearted smile. "In a manner of speaking, I guess I am."

It was obvious to Cole that there was a world of information left unsaid, but he couldn't pry any deeper. It was unusual for him to be so intrigued by a woman. Especially one he had just met. No doubt it was the lack of single women in town that was causing this unprecedented reaction. He really ought to excuse himself from the situation. He had no wish to make the poor woman uncomfortable. But watching the little girls playing together, he could see that Annie was still keeping part of her attention on the two adults, so he needed to keep Miss Jones there a little longer to ensure the child was properly settled.

"I never did get your answer about why you are so taken with the cleanliness out here in Missouri."

The woman's lips quirked into a crooked smile, as though she were contemplating an amusing answer. "Well, as I mentioned, I was actually prepared for Missouri to be dry and dusty, so I was expecting dirt and am therefore quite pleasantly surprised. But, unfortunately, while there are beautiful, clean parts of New York, I did not grow up in those neighborhoods. Where I lived was rather cramped and a little filthy, so I am quite enjoying the space here. And some of the illnesses in my neighborhood were thought to be caused by the water, so I always boiled any water I drank. It is a lovely experience to be able to drink cool water straight from the well in our backyard. It is one that Mrs. Carter and I appreciate every morning. I think it will take me quite a while to get to the point of taking that for granted."

Cole watched in fascination as she seemed to grow flustered. He rather thought it was from sharing such personal thoughts. His supposition was confirmed when she tried to turn the subject.

"But never mind about me. I'm a boring old tale. Please, Mr. Miller, tell me what brought you and your family to Bucklin."

Turning his gaze back to his daughter and away from his visitor's pretty features, Cole allowed his mind to drift back to the past.

"Despite growing up in a well-to-do family in the heart of Boston, I always craved making my own way in the world, as well as wider spaces than the city allowed for. I didn't want to follow in my older brother's footsteps into our father's business. I knew I'd always play second fiddle to Jonathan if I stayed."

The way she was nodding made him feel as though she could understand his sentiments. Warmth spread in his chest. He continued his tale.

"I was young and headstrong. I convinced our neighbor's daughter to join me in my westward adventures. I don't think she truly thought we'd stay here. She never fully understood my need to be free of my brother's shadow. I'm pretty sure Sheila expected us to have our little adventure here for at most a year or two. She thought I'd get tired of working so hard physically and would want to return to the city. But I had been completely honest with her before we married. I have no interest in being my brother's underling."

"Of course not, who would?" Her understanding made his throat feel tight. *Why couldn't Sheila have ever understood?* He shoved the unwelcome thought away.

"Anyway, I won't bore you with all the details. As it turned out, Sheila eventually tired of life here and her inability to convince me to return East."

Miss Jones's jaw dropped in suitably appropriate shock. "She left you?"

"In a manner of speaking." He echoed her earlier words. "She claimed she was just taking Mary home to meet her grandparents, but I suspected she wouldn't be returning. I didn't have the heart to deny her. I planned to follow her after a few weeks and bring her back. I expected she wouldn't enjoy the city as much as she had thought she would after having lived out here for a few years. But she caught a dreadful disease that had swept through the city and died within three weeks of her arrival. For all she thought life was safer in Boston, being closer to doctors, she would still be alive if she had stayed here."

The sympathy swimming in his guest's eyes nearly undid him. He cleared his throat and tried to muster a small smile. "Well, you are a remarkably good listener, I must say, Miss Jones. I almost never share this story with anyone, most certainly not with anyone I've just met."

"Well, I am honored that you shared your history with me." She glanced toward the children before fixing her bright gaze back on his. "But I must ask that you not share it with Annie. She is very sensitive to any talk of illness, which is why she is now with you, after all, since Mrs. Carter is helping the doctor with the Mitchells. Dr. Jeffries has not decided what exactly has befallen the Mitchells, but we fear it could be the influenza that swept New York."

"Of course. I do hope Mrs. Carter and the Mitchells will be all right."

His guest cast her worried gaze toward the children once more. "As do I. Can you imagine if the poor girl was to be orphaned again? It isn't to be considered. Katie is convinced she's immune to whatever has infected the Mitchells and she will return home before long, and I have chosen to believe her." She rose to her feet. "Mrs. Carter and I both appreciate your kindness in helping us out by keeping Annie distracted."

"Not at all. I didn't even know about your situation when we asked if Annie could stay over. Mary is thrilled to have a new friend. I'm just glad that it's turning out to be mutually beneficial."

The pretty woman's nerves seemed to be returning in force. She nodded with a tight smile on her face but didn't say anything more. She didn't even say goodbye to the little girl, just turned on her heel and left the house with half a wave as she hurried on her way. Cole watched her retreat wondering if it had been something he said.

Thinking back over their conversation, Cole couldn't imagine what would have made her take her leave so suddenly. While she had seemed nervous at first, he had thought she had warmed up to him as they shared a cup of coffee. Perhaps it was the discussion of his wife's death. No one likes to think about such a thing. Maybe she thought it was his fault. He couldn't blame her for that. He beat himself up over it all the time. If he had insisted she stay with him, she would still be alive. *But how was I supposed to do that?* She had been slowly turning into a misery, and he didn't want that infecting his little Mary. He had thought a trip back to Boston would have helped her see the advantages of their life in Missouri. There hadn't been time for that. She was dead before he had even boarded the train to come after them. At least he had gotten to Boston in time for her funeral. And blessedly, no one blamed him for her death, other than him. And Leandra had been willing to accompany him back to Bucklin to help with Mary.

His eyes strayed to his daughter as she played with her new little friend. His heart swelled as he watched her. Cole had never anticipated the love he was capable of. He had never loved anyone the way he loved his daughter. Certainly, no members of his family. Not even his wife, he hated to admit to himself. They had rubbed along well enough together at first, but her grumbling about their life in Missouri had chipped away at their friendship. *Why couldn't she have looked to the future instead of dwelling on the past?* He thought again of Miss Jones. She was clearly haunted by something but was trying to make the most of it. He really appreciated her positive attitude toward Missouri. No doubt, she would be married quickly in this town where single men abounded. He found he didn't quite like that idea.

Chapter Three

Melanie tried to slow her steps but couldn't quite manage a sedate pace as she hurried back to the safety and comfort of the small white house she and Katie called home. She was torn between pride and despair over her encounter with Mr. Miller. It was the longest conversation she had shared with anyone other than Katie in months. And she had actually enjoyed it, for the most part. But then her fears had returned, and she had felt the need to flee his presence as though the hounds of hell were nipping at her heels. No doubt the man would think her an imbecile. Or just one more foolish female. Surely the poor man had had his fill of them. *He would probably like Katie*, she thought with a stab of irrational jealousy.

She tried to shake the negative thoughts from her mind by literally shaking her head and turning her attention outward. Castigating herself for her feelings had never helped in the past, so she wasn't going to continue. *Look at the vast, blue sky*, she reminded herself. *Breathe in that clean, fresh air. Feast your eyes on the vibrant green and yellow of the fields out behind the main street of the new little town. Ignore the dull gray of the little houses that line that main street. What does it matter if no one has planted any roses? Why don't you do it? Write to Mrs. Parker at the orphanage in New York and ask that she send you some cuttings with the next shipment of orphans.*

Her breathing and her footsteps slowed to a normal rhythm as she calmed her thoughts and neared her home. She dearly loved the little house she and Katie were renting. And she was so proud of the little business they were running. Thus calmed, she turned her thoughts to the sewing she would work on that afternoon. With Annie suitably settled and Katie otherwise occupied, Melanie thought she should be able to get quite a bit done as the hours stretched ahead of her with no one to demand anything of her. It was a heady feeling to be mistress of her own life.

For fifteen years she had felt the heavy burden of responsibility. She had been only ten years old when her mother had died within days of birthing Henry. Their father hadn't known what to do with the baby and his three-year-old daughter, so he had let his ten-year-old daughter take it all on. She had essentially become a mother at the age of ten. Now she was twenty-five. Her father had recently died and left everything to Henry. He was going through a rather obnoxious phase and no longer needed her. Sweet little Claudia was married and also no longer needed her. Melanie was relieved that Claudia had married a pleasant young man from a big, loving family. Claudia would be well taken care of if she needed anything. So, Melanie was free to get on with her new life. If only she could get over her issues from her old life, things would be perfect.

She stepped through her door with a sigh of relief then leaned against the door while surveying the tidy kitchen of their small home. She and Katie had done very well for themselves when they'd arranged for its rental. It was hard for her to fathom that someone had willingly moved out of the pretty little house. To Melanie's mind, there was nowhere better than the four walls holding up the sturdy roof. She loved living in a house. Never again would she willingly live in a tenement. While there were certain conveniences in living so crowded up with others, they were far outweighed by the drawbacks, in her opinion. If she never smelled another home's cooking, it would be too soon, she thought fiercely as she took an appreciative, deep inhale of the fresh scent lingering in the air. She had left the windows open when she left with Annie, and there were no lingering odors from the breakfast she had cooked that morning. It was wonderful. She couldn't remove the grin from her face. No one was about so she didn't even try.

Thinking back to the home she had grown up in, Melanie couldn't quite suppress the shudder that shivered down her spine. The tight quarters in the tenement building had seemed luxurious when they had first moved in. The landlord had made an effort to make the building attractive. But now, being out here in all the space that Missouri had to offer, Melanie couldn't bear to think of the three rooms that had made up the apartment she had shared with her younger siblings and their father. And they had been lucky. With only four of them, and none of them trying to run a business from home, they weren't nearly as crowded as some of their neighbors. Many of the other apartments housed five, six, even seven people in the same space that they were cramped with four. And then some of the ladies in the building were taking in sewing so they needed to keep one of the rooms presentable for any customers who might come around.

That was, of course, how Melanie had learned to sew. Mrs. Becker had been kind enough to teach her and then give her a job. She had been so proud of herself for helping her father support the family. Little did she know how little value he had placed upon her efforts. Melanie shoved the unwelcome thought hastily away. It wouldn't help her efforts at calmness if she thought about her childhood, even if thinking of Mrs. Becker was a highlight in her life.

Melanie took a few more deep breaths of the fresh, sweet-smelling air that flowed through her open windows and then set to the tasks before her. She began to hum a song that Mrs. Becker had always sung while they worked together. It kept the smile she had forced onto her lips in place. Within minutes it was no longer fake — she was happy doing her work.

Hours flew by and before she knew it, Melanie found herself in a darkened room with a finished garment. She grinned with satisfaction. There was nothing quite like the deep satisfaction she felt every time she remembered how far she'd come. She looked around in the gloom but felt not an ounce of fear. Everything here was hers, or hers and Katie's. There was no one to tell her what to do; no one would be able to take this away from her. She knew her smile was stretching her face, but she didn't care. There was no one about to try to tell her how she ought to be feeling and no one to censure her for looking silly as she grinned at nothing in particular.

Bustling about, Melanie put the sewing materials away after lighting the lamp. It wouldn't do to keep stitching. She had gotten to the point in the garment that finer work was needed. She would wait until the sun would illuminate her handiwork.

Bright and early the next morning Melanie was up and back at work, but the back of her mind niggled. She loved having the house to herself and all her newfound independence. But she had come to care about Katie, and she was worried about her being cooped up in the sick house under quarantine.

Guilt was uppermost on her mind, if Melanie was being truly honest. It was only because of her own insecurities that Katie was the one who had to visit their patrons. If Katie hadn't called to see Mrs. Mitchell to get her measurements, she wouldn't be stuck there trying to help them get well. Of course, if Katie hadn't been there, the Mitchells might be dead already. But it wasn't really fair that all the visits fell to Katie to make. In all actuality, it should have been at least a fifty percent chance of Melanie being stuck there with them. She shuddered at the thought. Katie was far more equipped for such a hideous situation, in Melanie's opinion.

Of course, the poor dear can't be enjoying being stuck with the good doctor, Melanie thought with a sly grin. *I think she protests about him a little too much.* Of course, given her background, Melanie couldn't blame the young woman overmuch. But anyone with eyes could see that the two were attracted to each other. *I wonder how many sparks are flying in that house?* Melanie hadn't seen the inside of the Mitchells' house, but from the outside it looked like it would be close quarters. Katie had looked exhausted when Melanie had seen her the day before. She really did wish there was something she could do to help the situation other than bring food. But Katie had been right when she said there was no use in them all being exposed.

With a sigh, Melanie set to baking. At least she could bring Katie and the Mitchells a meal. The patients might not be up to eating much, but the caregivers had to keep their strength up. *And then I'll finish that frock I was working on,* Melanie thought. *At the very least, I can make sure we meet our business obligations while Katie is stuck with the doctor.* With another, softer sigh Melanie thought of Annie and Mr. Miller. Melanie would have to make sure the little girl was kept occupied.

She determined to call round to Katie with the food and decide whether or not Annie needed to stay away a little longer. Mary's father seemed like a kind enough gentleman. If need be, he would probably keep the youngster another night.

Some time later, Melanie was surprised to feel a spring in her step as she walked away from the Mitchells' home. It made no sense for her to be feeling sprightly. She was worried about Katie and dreading speaking to the handsome Mr. Miller. Wasn't she? Of course, she was, Melanie reminded herself. She was just hurrying out of concern for Annie. She managed not to even roll her eyes at her own foolishness.

Chapter Four

By the time she approached the Cole residence, Melanie could see Mr. Miller working out in one of his paddocks. It seemed as though he was training a horse. She had never seen such an activity before, and the breath caught in her throat as the scene played out in front of her.

Melanie's city-bred sentiments had never thought much of horses. If she had thought of them, it would have only been to consider them slightly terrifying but useful, as they pulled the wagons and carriages that filled the streets of New York. But now, as she watched the powerful animal being trained by the handsome man, she found the scene moving, beautiful, even breath-taking. And it wasn't only because Mr. Miller had removed his shirt in the gathering heat of the day. As the horse tossed its head and pranced around at the end of its tether; it seemed to Melanie as though the beautiful animal was flirting with the man. She couldn't tear her gaze away and only realized she was holding her breath when Mr. Miller finally noticed her. When he raised his hand in a wave, the air whooshed out of her in a gasp. Thankfully, he was far enough away that he couldn't possibly have heard, but Melanie felt the heat creeping up her cheeks anyway. She tried to keep her face neutral, but she was rather afraid that a sheepish smile was stretching her cheeks. With relief, she saw that he likely realised his state of undress and was quickly buttoning up his shirt as she walked toward him.

"Good morning, Miss Jones," Mr. Miller called as she approached.

Melanie was having serious second thoughts about coming out to his property. She wished she could undo the last half hour of her life. She should have returned home after seeing Katie. But instead she was standing still, looking at the handsome man. *Gaping really, if I'm going to be perfectly honest*, she thought with a cringe. Nothing could be done but to brave through the awkward moment.

"Morning, Mr. Miller."

"Are you here to collect Annie? I thought she would be staying through the day."

Even with a frown creasing his face, the man still managed to steal her breath. Melanie wondered if she were getting ill or losing her mind.

"Actually, sir, as it turns out, Katie is going to be staying with the Mitchells a little longer, so I was stopping in to see how Annie had fared and to see if we might prevail upon your hospitality a little longer."

"It has been a pleasure having the wee lass with us, I can assure you."

Melanie couldn't look him in the eye as he answered her for fear he would see just how compelling she found him. He misinterpreted her focus.

"Fond of the horses, are you, miss?"

Melanie felt the color rising in her cheeks anew. She started to stammer a reply. "Well, this one is certainly handsome."

"That she is," he agreed. "She might prefer you to say she's pretty, but she appreciates any compliment headed in her direction."

Melanie's eyes flew to meet his gaze. She was mortified to realize he was teasing her. The color staining her cheeks now spread to engulf her entire face and neck. She wanted to fan her face to try to cool down but didn't want to draw any more attention to her discomfort. So, she attempted to turn the subject.

"Does she have a name?"

"Not as yet." He was watching Melanie as though she were a fascinating specimen. "It's my turn to come up with a name, but I haven't been able to think of anything yet. For now, we've been referring to her as the new foal but since we've got pregnant mares, I really need to get on with it."

Despite how awkward Melanie felt, she couldn't help laughing over his words. "I guess that will get confusing soon."

He turned his interested gaze back from the horse and focused on her. "Do you have some suggestions? I swear, I'm clear out of ideas."

"Oh, well, no, I wouldn't have the first clue where to start." Melanie stumbled out her reply. Turning her focus back to the animal, she marvelled. "Is she really just a baby?"

"Well, I'm ashamed to say, she's actually heading for two years old. We haven't had any of our mares breeding for a while as we've been focusing our attention on other endeavors. I've clearly been putting off the task of naming her." He scratched the foal's head as the animal leaned into him. "I'm growing too fond of the young lady, and I'm trying to keep from getting too attached. I think I've been putting off the task of naming her in the hopes that it'll prevent me from falling completely in love."

Melanie giggled. "Would that be so terrible? I've never known anyone to complain about being in love."

"When you plan to sell the object of your affections, it's a terrible idea."

Melanie's face fell. "Oh dear. I can see how that would be uncomfortable. This must be a serious disadvantage to your line of work. What shall you do?"

"Do you want to name her? That might help. Then it wouldn't be me that did it, so maybe my heart won't become quite so engaged."

Joy and dread intermingled in Melanie's heart. She had never been able to name anything. She had always allowed the children to name any pets they had acquired through the years. And of course, her mother had named the children, even little Henry, just before she died. But what a huge responsibility. And she didn't want to love the horse either. What good would that be to her poor abused heart?

"Oh, well, I don't know how I could possibly," she began to stumble out a response again.

"Well, at least think on it," the rancher replied, saving her from her discomfort. "Seeing as you're here, but you're planning to leave Annie with us, why don't you stay and spend some time? You can watch Baby Foal a bit and see if you have any ideas for names. And I'm certain Leandra would be glad for some company. She was mighty disappointed that she missed you when you called yesterday."

Melanie had been envisioning another quiet day alone, but she felt churlish to refuse.

"That's kind of you to say, sir."

"Not kind at all, it's the truth. Most of the reason Leandra wants to return East is because she's pining for the company of other adult females. You'd be doing us a mighty big favor if you would bide a while."

Now there was no way she could refuse. She could feel that her smile was a little weak, but she offered it anyway as she answered, "It would be a pleasure, in that case."

He nodded abruptly, and Melanie wondered if she ought to excuse herself from his presence. Why was she always so awkward? What was she supposed to do? She wasn't sure if her desperate questions were written on her face, but he answered them anyway.

"Would you like to help with her training while you think of a name? Leandra is probably just getting up so she won't be ready for a visit for a spell."

Melanie was surprised at the offer, yet her awkwardness eased slightly. Not that she had the first clue what she could possibly have to say to the man, she thought, even as she fought the urge to brush the lock of hair back from his brow as it fell down with his movements.

Again, he alleviated her discomfort. "You said you don't have much experience with horses. Does that mean you've never ridden?"

She shook her head. "My father bought a pair of horses to pull his carriage a few years ago, but I didn't have anything to do with the care of them. We couldn't even keep them where we lived. He had to board them at the livery stables. And I didn't even ride in the carriage all that often."

He looked at her strangely but didn't pry. She felt the flush creeping back into her face. "The carriage was for taking him to visit his customers, not for my use. I needed to stay home with the children, anyway."

As though he could tell there was much she left out in her explanation, he again didn't pry, for which she was deeply grateful. It was all she could do to bear up under the searching glance he cast her, as though he were assessing her thoughts.

"It doesn't much matter if you're experienced or not, but try not to be afraid. Horses can sense it, and it makes them skittish."

"Telling me not to be afraid doesn't really do much to alleviate my fears, sir."

His chuckle set the butterflies fluttering in her belly. "I can see why you would say that, and I apologize." He produced a carrot from his back pocket. "She's been after this all morning. You can make fast friends with her by offering it to her." He showed Melanie how to hold her hand in a safe way to offer the treat to the large animal.

Melanie was fascinated with the softness of the horse's nose. "Can I pet her?"

"Of course. She'll love you forever if you scratch her here between her ears. But gently. Horses' ears are very flexible and sensitive. It's a large part of why they can be so skittish. They have keen eyesight and hearing, so they can be easily frightened."

"Hello, lovely," Melanie crooned as the animal tried to cuddle with her, butting her head against her chest. She couldn't prevent her giggle despite the fact the large animal's affection nearly knocked her over. The rancher's answering grin sent shivers down Melanie's spine.

Part of her found the experience stimulating and delicious. But another part of her wished she had stayed home. Melanie could feel her face tightening as she tried to think of something to say, but her mind was a blank. Not to mention, the flutters in her stomach were not at all pleasant, and she fought for breath.

"Now that you've made friends, do you think you could hold onto her lead while I get the saddle?"

"What?" she squeaked. "How could you possibly think I could hold on to her if she has a mind to leave? In case you haven't noticed, there's a significant size difference between us."

The slow grin he offered as he cast an assessing gaze over her and the horse made her take another step back.

"As a matter of fact, I did happen to notice that you're no bigger than a tadpole." Melanie blinked at his comparison, but he carried on. "But it won't make a difference. Now that Baby Foal has decided that you're her friend, she'll stay with you. Besides, despite their sharp vision, or maybe because of it, she doesn't really realize how very little you are. Horses are remarkably obedient animals. Unless she gets spooked by something, she will listen to whatever you have to say. Of course, the saddle might spook her, so I'll stay close by."

Melanie didn't find his words overly reassuring, but she was of the opinion that she would die of embarrassment if she walked away before she died of injuries if she stayed, so she forced her feet to stay still and took the leather lead he handed her.

Before she realized it, time had passed without too much awkwardness. Melanie was ridiculously proud of herself as she continued to stand still, talking softly to the horse as Mr. Miller had slowly, gently placed the saddle on her back. The horse had shuffled her feet, flicked her ears and tail, and tossed her head a little, but she had tolerated the pressure. Mr. Miller had also crooned soft words of encouragement to the large animal to keep her aware of his presence and comfort her as well. Melanie had found it comforting too and had to work at keeping her eyes away from him.

Finally, Mr. Miller removed the saddle, took the lead off the horse's head, and turned her free with a gentle slap on her rump. Without the horse between them, Melanie was once again left feeling tongue tied.

"You were of great help, Miss Jones, thank you so much for your assistance." He paused as though waiting for her to reply, but all she could do was bob her head bashfully and look away. "Have you been able to think of any ideas for her name or were you too busy telling her stories?"

Melanie knew he was teasing her, but she was swamped with mortification. She had forgotten he was listening and had just been spouting foolish nonsense to the horse. Melanie wanted the ground to swallow her but struggled for coherent thought in case that didn't conveniently happen.

Clearing her throat helped her get words starting to flow. "All the ideas I've thought of are rather too obvious and trite. For example, I thought Star for the white marking on her forehead or Boots for the white on her legs. Or Brownie for the obvious reason of her color. But she seems to be too special for a mundane name. We could maybe come up with something from the Latin equus or caballus. Or even Aethon might be a good name. It's still for the marking on her forehead but far more interesting than Star. Of course, it might be a male name. If we're going to stick with Latin we could go with Gemmula and call her Gem for short since, she really is a jewel."

Melanie was starting to feel like she was babbling and wished she could bite off her tongue. She managed to rein it in, and silence fell between them. "You probably shouldn't have asked me," she muttered. "All my ideas are ridiculous."

"Not a single one of them was ridiculous," he said in a firm tone. "Technically, the marking on her head is neither a star nor a blaze. In horse description, it's more like a stripe. But I still like all your name suggestions. I'm just surprised to find you are a scholar."

Melanie could feel the color ebbing and flowing in her face as she had paled in her mortification, but now hot embarrassment swept her. "I'm no scholar. Unfortunately, I didn't have much opportunity for schooling."

"Well then, how do you know Latin?" He sounded incredulous.

Melanie shrugged and offered an awkward chuckle. "I like to read. And learn. My brother went to school, and I had to help him with his studies."

When she finally glanced to his face for a brief moment, she was amazed to see that he appeared impressed, but she rejected her own observation and cast her gaze away. She must have been mistaken.

"Did your brother do well in school?"

"Fairly well," she answered, "when I could prevail upon him to sit still and do his studies. He couldn't see any sense in learning something like Latin, since he always knew he would be going into business with our father. Thankfully, he understood the need for mathematics, so that was far less of a struggle."

"You know your maths, too?"

Melanie shrugged again. "Somewhat." She was much too uncomfortable to discuss it further. "Do you think your sister might be ready to receive yet?"

"Oh, why yes, she probably is. I plumb forgot you were waiting to see her." He turned and began to lead her toward the house. "Come along, Annie will want to see you as well." He stopped in his tracks after a few strides and Melanie, hurrying to keep up with him, almost collided with him. As it was, she had to put out her hand to steady herself and encountered the tight muscles of his upper arm. She marveled at his strength even as she was pulling her hand back and trying to look anywhere else but him.

"Sorry to be so clumsy, Miss Jones," he apologized, even though it was her that hadn't been watching where she was going. "But I just thought of something in connection with Annie. If possible, it would be best if the girls think it's their idea for Annie to stay longer if you don't want her to realize there's something amiss with her mother."

Melanie, her mind still preoccupied with the man's physique, found her thoughts to be slow to catch up to his words. When she finally realized what he was getting at, she was impressed with his reasoning. "That's brilliant, sir, but how would we arrange that?"

"It shouldn't be too hard, my Mary doesn't have friends sleep over often, but when she does, she never wants their time together to end."

Chapter Five

Cole had never enjoyed a morning of horse training more. Even his late wife hadn't been quite so fascinating, he thought before chiding himself for such disloyal musings. But the young woman, he interrupted himself in his thoughts as he looked at her a bit closer. She wasn't exactly so young, he realized upon closer inspection. Her innocence and lack of experience made him think of her as young, but he could see that she must be in her mid-twenties. The perfect age, if you asked him. He had been in his mid-twenties as well when he had first come to Missouri and staked his claim on the land. He had returned to Boston to marry his wife, but his heart had belonged in the West for the last ten years.

He had loved his Sheila, of course. But it had been difficult living with someone who was so dissatisfied with the life they had chosen together. Cole stifled his sigh. The past was the past and needed to remain there. His attention returned to the conversation in front of him.

As he had suspected, Leandra was thrilled to have female company and was nearly talking Miss Jones' ear off. Cole grinned as he watched their visitor blinking at the onslaught of words headed her way. The pretty new arrival to town was clearly not dimwitted. She quickly realized that Leandra had plenty to say and didn't require a response, despite the questions she was asking. He was fascinated to see what he thought might be the first genuine smile to grace her face as Miss Jones seemed to relax subtly. The poor woman seemed to be a nervous little thing despite her professed delight to be in Missouri.

Cole wondered if he ought to leave the women to themselves, but he didn't get much company either, and he didn't have any pressing chores to care for, so he wanted to enjoy the visitor, too. Besides, he reminded himself, he had promised to help the little girls think it was their idea for Annie to stay. Thus reassured, he settled in to enjoy his tea.

Being well versed in his sister's stories and complaints, Cole didn't pay too close attention to her words, contenting himself with shifting his attention between the window that looked out over his land and their visitor's expressive face. If he had been questioned, he wouldn't have been able to say which view gave him more pleasure.

It was obvious Miss Jones wasn't completely comfortable. He wondered what had made her so awkward. It seemed to go in waves with the poor woman. When she forgot about herself, she was able to get beyond her issues, and conversation flowed freely, but when she grew self-conscious, she became tied for words. He was happy to see her relax into the flow of Leandra's words. Before his sister ran out of things to say, though, the two little girls spilled into the room, a jumble of small limbs, giggles, and exuberant energy. They tumbled to a stop when they spotted Miss Jones.

"Hello, Miss Jones." Cole was proud of his daughter for her polite greeting.

"Hello, Mary. Are you having a nice time with Annie?"

The little girl nodded vigorously while her gaze shifted between her father and their visitor. "You aren't here to take Annie away already are you?" she blurted out before biting her lip in indecision as she glanced at her father. "I'm sorry to be rude. But we're having lots of fun. And Annie really loves the puppies, don't you Annie?"

The other little girl looked nervously around the room, uncertainty written clearly on her petite features. Cole was surprised when Miss Jones quickly set the child at ease.

"Good morning, Annie, dear, how are you? I don't mean to interrupt your time with your friend. I just wanted to be certain that you were comfortable here, as you haven't slept over before."

It was the right thing to say for the little girl's face split into a wide smile and she nodded vigorously. "Oh, Miss Melanie, I'm having a grand time. We've been careful not to get hurt like the last time I played over at Suzie's place."

Miss Jones laughed. "Well, that's certainly a relief."

"Is that why you came to check on me?"

Miss Jones blinked. Cole was heartened by the observation that she clearly didn't want to lie to the little girl. "I just wanted to be sure that all was well." Cole had to rub his chin to disguise his amusement over her tactful answer. Despite not having her own offspring, she was clearly used to managing children.

The little girl took her answer in stride. She nodded acceptance. "You must come see the puppies."

"Are they absolutely darling?" Miss Jones asked, giving her attention completely to the little girls, including Mary in her question.

The two children were talking over each other, eager to share their tales with a receptive adult. Much to Cole's regret, Leandra didn't appreciate being cut out of the visitor's attention and soon interrupted.

"Girls, why don't you go back outside to play? We grownups are still finishing our tea."

Cole bit the edge of his tongue to prevent a smile from creasing his face as he watched Miss Jones absorb his sister's rudeness toward the children. She offered the little girls a kind smile.

"I'll join you outside shortly, and you can show me the puppies." Cole was impressed that she was so diplomatic. She didn't contradict the other adult, but she didn't exclude the children either.

Mary shifted from foot to foot as she looked expectantly at her father. "I'm not done playing with Annie, Papa. Can she stay over another night?"

Cole was pleased to see the other child's eyes light up. Obviously, Annie wasn't averse to the idea of staying another night. "Let Miss Jones and I talk about it, and I'll let you know, all right? When she comes out to see the puppies she'll tell you if Annie can stay longer."

He watched as his daughter's face fell, but he didn't want to give away that it had already been planned. He was fairly sure it was the right way of handling it and was pleased to watch as the visitor bent low and whispered to Annie. He could only guess that she was checking with the child to make sure she was agreeable to staying longer. Her vigorous nod to the affirmative set him at ease. He was surprised to feel anticipation toward the woman's next visit when she hadn't even left yet from this one.

Cole was feeling quite content until he glanced back toward his sister. Her face looked thunderous. Leandra was not pleased that the children hadn't yet left the room. Hoping to avoid an altercation, he quickly shooed the girls away. "Run along now, girls. Miss Jones will join you shortly."

With their giggles trailing behind them, the youngsters clattered from the room.

"Well now, where were we?" Leandra asked before resuming her monologue.

Cole contented himself with watching Miss Jones' face. He was relieved to see that while a myriad of feelings chased themselves across her features, uppermost appeared to be amusement. Rather than being offended by his sister's rudeness toward the children, it would appear she was accustomed to it and found it funny rather than off putting. Finally, his sister got to an interesting point.

"Well, Miss Jones, I must say, you are an exceptional conversationalist," his sister said, which caused their visitor to chuckle.

"That's terribly kind of you to say, Miss Miller." Miss Jones sounded sincere despite her amusement.

"But I don't think you have told me very much about yourself," Leandra observed. "How do you come to find yourself in this backward place? Surely you won't be staying for very long."

Cole watched as Miss Jones struggled to answer her question. She was too polite to contradict her hostess, but he was fairly certain she didn't consider Bucklin to be so very backward.

"Actually, Miss Miller," she began before being interrupted.

"Oh, you really must call me Leandra. We absolutely must be friends. I am so very glad to have another woman nearby."

Miss Jones' smile was warm. "Thank you, Leandra, I would be happy to be friends. And you must call me Melanie."

"Very well, Melanie. Tell me, what brought you to this dreadful place?"

Cole's gut clenched as he watched the pretty woman bite her lip before answering. Her smile was tentative as she began. "Actually, I haven't yet found anything to be dreadful since I arrived." Her tone was apologetic but firm. "My friend and I were volunteers at an orphanage in New York City and were assigned the task of accompanying a trainload of the orphans, who were coming out West to join new families here. We had already accompanied children on the trains a few times, but we felt that this time it was going to also be our turn to start new lives."

"Isn't your family terribly disappointed to have you so far away?"

"I don't have any family that needs me." Her answer was simple but stark. "My mother has been gone for fifteen years. She died giving birth to my brother. My father died a year ago. In between my brother and me, I have a sister. She married six months ago. Life with my brother was no longer bearable, so I decided to get a fresh start here in Missouri."

"Oh, my dear, I am right sorry." Despite her selfish ways, Leandra still had a kind heart and hadn't intended to dredge up painful thoughts for her new friend.

"Don't be sorry, Leandra. It just is what it is. Mrs. Carter and I are having a fine time getting settled and starting up our seamstress business. She is delighted to have her new daughter, and I am happy to have a life of my own."

Leandra nodded although she didn't look as though she believed their guest. But she didn't dwell on it for very long. She launched into her own thoughts, which Miss Jones politely listened to for a few more minutes before she rose to her feet.

"It has been such a pleasure to make your acquaintance, Leandra, and I thank you for your hospitality. But I really mustn't keep you from your chores any longer, and I ought to be on my way."

Again, Cole stifled his amusement as his sister looked confused. She didn't do very much around his spread, so there weren't many chores she would be doing once their guest left. He was surprised to see amusement twinkling in Miss Jones' eyes as though she knew what he was thinking.

"Thank you so much, again, for keeping Annie another night. Mrs. Carter is anxious to keep the child from worrying about her absence. Having her here is an excellent distraction. Hopefully, Annie needn't ever know that her mom hasn't been at home. I'm just so grateful that she wasn't suspicious why it was me checking on her rather than her mother."

"I'm just as glad to have Mary occupied as well, so we might as well say that it's a mutual favor," Leandra answered. "Do promise you'll stay for another tea when you come round to collect the child."

Miss Jones smiled but didn't completely accept. "Perhaps you'll have the pleasure of making the acquaintance of Annie's mother. I'll be sure to tell her to plan for tea if it's she who comes to collect Annie."

Leandra looked pleased at the prospect of another visitor as she followed her to the door. "Either way, don't be a stranger."

Cole accompanied Miss Jones as she stepped out onto the porch. Leandra appeared to be torn. She wanted to prolong her time with their visitor, but she didn't like to be around the animals. When she saw that Melanie was heading toward the barn, she stepped back into the house.

"I'm sorry about my sister," Cole began but was quickly cut off by a flash of what looked like anger in Miss Jones' face.

"You needn't apologize for her. Your sister is a dear."

Cole was taken aback and frowned. "I wouldn't describe her in that way, myself."

"Well you ought to. Didn't you say she came out her to help you with your daughter when your wife passed?"

He sputtered a little bit but didn't know how to reply. She carried on, all trace of awkwardness gone, at least for the moment. "Your gratitude should make you see that she has left all that is comfortable for her, and she is struggling just like everyone else. She is a dear," Melanie repeated, her firm tone brooking no argument.

Cole grinned. "I see you're the type who thinks all women should be loyal to each other."

His words seemed to deflate her inexplicable anger, and she offered him a weak grin. "I am, yes. It might make me a little unreasonable at times."

With a shrug and a nod Cole admitted, "Maybe so, but I think it's admirable anyway. And since I love my sister despite her ways, I appreciate your loyalty on her behalf." They walked in silence for a beat before he added, "And you needn't thank us for keeping Annie. As you might have noticed, Leandra doesn't have all that much patience for noisy play, so it's good for Mary to have company to be able to play out of doors. I think she sometimes finds it boring to try to play by herself all the time despite what an imagination the girl has."

Miss Jones nodded but looked uncomfortable once more. Cole was relieved they had reached the barn and could hear the girls playing in an empty stall.

Cole was impressed once more when she kept her voice low but called out to the girls. "Hello? I'm here to see the puppies." She had the sense not to disturb the animals even if she hadn't been on a farm before.

The two giggling girls called from the stall they were in. "Over here, Miss Melanie."

When they reached the partition, Cole watched Melanie's face rather than looking in. He was quite familiar with his daughter's appearance and had already spent time with the puppies himself, so he wanted to enjoy the woman's first experience with the young animals. He was so glad he did. The wonder and joy that spread across her face as she watched the little girls playing with the wriggling balls of fur was a pleasure to behold. It was obvious the woman had a deep sense of inner peace despite her occasional social awkwardness.

"Aren't they the most darling things you've ever seen, Miss Melanie?"

"That they are, Annie," the woman promptly replied. "But doesn't their mother mind you playing with her babies?" She was obviously a worrier.

"No," Mary answered simply.

This was obviously not enough of an answer for Miss Jones. She turned a face full of inquiry toward Cole, and he quickly soothed her concerns. "The puppies' mother is a sweet, gentle dog that we've had since Mary was a baby. She's quite used to Mary's attentions. And this is her third litter of puppies, so she isn't a nervous mother."

"But they look so tiny. Are you certain the girls won't hurt them?"

Cole grinned at her hushed tone. He wasn't sure if she was trying to avoid hurting the children's feelings or if she didn't want to disturb the puppies. He found it endearing.

"Puppies are tough despite how little they look. But they actually aren't so very young. It's not as though they were just born. They are already almost three weeks old. They can't stray far from their mother, but it won't hurt them to socialize with the girls."

Cole grinned when she turned her attention back to the puppies after she had searched his gaze for confirmation of his sincerity. It seemed to him as though her gaze on the little dogs was full of longing.

"Would you like to hold one yourself?"

"Oh, no, I couldn't possibly."

He chuckled softly. "Is that your response to everything?"

Her cheeks turned pink, and she looked mortified as she turned to him but then quickly cast her gaze to the ground in a bashful manner. Cole felt bad for teasing her. He quickly reminded her, "It's what you said about helping me with the foal, and about naming the horse."

Her cheeks remained brightly colored, but comprehension flooded her face. "I've never held a puppy before. Any animals we ever had were stray cats my brother or sister found. Cats, when they finally allow you to handle them, are either watchful and guarded or relaxed and prone. Those little balls of fur look like they would wiggle right out of your hands if you aren't very careful."

Cole could see that she had actually given the matter some thought, and he felt even worse about teasing her. "Why don't you sit down on that overturned pail, then you'll be able to hold the pup in your lap. I'll grab one from the girls for you."

He couldn't help smiling as the woman looked nervous but eager while he grabbed what he hopped was the least squirmy of the litter. When their hands connected as he settled the warm bundle in her lap, Cole felt a jolt that he quickly fought to ignore. It suddenly dawned on him that he was attracted to the pretty woman, and that just wouldn't do. She obviously had emotional issues to which he wasn't privy. And he had enough emotional females on his hands with his bitter sister and motherless daughter. He didn't need another one, no matter how soft and sweet she seemed or how kind she was as she crooned gently to the small animal cradled in her hands.

❧❧❧

Melanie stared down at the brown ball of fluff in her lap. She was holding a puppy! The one thing her sister had always wished for, she thought wistfully before a grin split her face when the little animal started to lick and chew on her fingers. In that instant, Melanie's heart melted. How would she live without the warm little bundle in her life? She quickly chastised herself for the ridiculous thought. *You've managed to reach the ripe old age of twenty-five without ever once having a puppy in your life. You can certainly live through the experience of playing with one for a moment and then giving him back.*

But oh, how she didn't want to return the little creature. Not that she had any need for such a complication, she reminded herself. *Just think of how you reacted when Katie said she wanted to adopt Annie. You thought the younger woman was foolish. And now, you wish you could have a dog? You scoop this little bundle up and return him right this minute, Melanie Jones!* The silent lecture didn't help her very much. She scooped up the little animal but instead of handing him back to the rancher, she cuddled it closer to her chest, a sense of peace permeating her as the puppy licked her once more and then settled down as though it were going to sleep. Melanie was so surprised she didn't know what to make of the development.

She blinked and met Mr. Miller's gaze as he watched attentively. Melanie wondered if he was worried she would hurt the animal. His smile did disconcerting things to her tummy while also assuring her he wasn't overly worried about the pup.

"I think the girls tuckered him out before we even got here. I hope you aren't disappointed that he isn't a little more playful."

Melanie was pretty sure her gaze was full of longing as she returned it to the sleeping animal. "Not at all. He's almost as restful as a purring cat."

"Do you prefer cats?" His tone led her to think he wasn't as impressed with her preferences.

She shrugged. "I wouldn't say I prefer them. I just have never held a dog before. We did have cats, though. In the city, it wasn't uncommon to have rodents invade. It was always a challenge to have a balanced animal – one that was able to hunt, but also would willingly accept the affections of my little sister and brother."

Again the man grinned, and the flutter it caused in her chest made Melanie surge to her feet while being careful not to disturb the sleeping puppy. "I really ought to be going," she stated firmly without meeting Mr. Miller's gaze. "Annie, if you're sure you want to stay another day,

I will let your mother know that you are behaving nicely and having a good time."

"Thank you, Miss Melanie," the child answered politely despite being preoccupied.

Melanie was amused by the youngster but felt her smile fading as she turned to Mr. Miller to take her leave. "Thank you so much for your assistance, sir. Mrs. Carter and I are both very grateful."

"I told you, no thanks necessary. I appreciate Mary having a little friend to play with."

"Very well, then." Melanie needed to be brusque in order to excuse herself. "I will wish you a good day, then, Mr. Miller." She gently passed the puppy into his large hands, turned on her heel, and marched out of the barn without a backward glance.

Chapter Six

Melanie was berating herself every step of the way home. *How could you be so ridiculous as to go and get all aflutter about a handsome man? You are surely much too old for such nonsense. It's not as though you have any interest in pursuing a courtship with him. He's a father, for land's sakes! The father of a girl child besides, so you can be sure he'll be after having a son. No, Miss Melanie Jones, you are to get all thoughts of handsome ranchers with deep voices and cleft chins out of your head. You are a senseless woman who can barely leave the house. What you do not need is fluttery feelings about a man.*

Trying to cast her thoughts elsewhere, Melanie thought about the animals she had seen while visiting the Miller place. The horses had been magnificent. Having so rarely been that close to one, she hadn't realized just how majestic the beasts were. No wonder most people were mad about them, she thought with a wry twist of her lips. Perhaps she and Katie ought to think of getting a gig or carriage of some sort and a lovely horse to pull it. It would certainly make Katie's task of visiting their customers much easier. Of course, if you have a horse, you have to know how to care for it. Melanie shuddered slightly. She didn't think she could cope with the responsibility. It was best to think of something other than the lovely creatures she had spent time with, she decided with a little shake of her head.

She forced her mind to the tasks ahead of her. She still had several hours of good light, so she should be able to get ahead in their work. If Katie wasn't home soon, Melanie would be fully caught up, and her partner would have to go visiting right away to make the deliveries and take the measurements for more orders.

A stirring of guilt marred her thoughts as she settled in to her labors. Maybe it wasn't fair to Katie that she was the one who had to face all the customers. *But if I'm pulling my full share of the sewing, or even more than my share, then surely it balances out, doesn't it?* Katie had certainly never complained. She even said she enjoys the visits. Except for that time a couple days ago when she visited Mrs. Jenkins and the poor old woman fainted on Katie. That wasn't comfortable for either of them.

Thinking of that mishap caused Melanie to begin speculating about Katie and the doctor. They sure had ended up in one another's company many times recently. *I think Katie protests a trifle too much when I tease her about Doctor Jeffries. Perhaps I shouldn't be doing that though,* Melanie mused. *It's not as though I'm anxious to be rid of her. If she marries, that would leave me in an awkward position. I might have to face the customers for myself.* Melanie's stomach clenched, and it felt as though her heart skipped a beat or two. *More thoughts that cannot be borne,* she thought with frustration. *I really ought to figure out how to deal with people once more. But not today,* she argued with herself as she caught sight of her small house. She had dealt sufficiently with enough people for one day. *With how handsome Mr. Miller is, surely that encounter must count for more than one person. And now you're keeping score?* She mocked herself silently.

Shoving all the disquieting thoughts to the side, Melanie set to work. She was soon caught up in her project and relaxed into her tasks. The time flew by and before she knew it, it was too dark to see. As she put everything away and fastened her windows tight, the thought skittered through her mind that she didn't love being completely alone at night. *You really ought to try to dissuade Katie from a potential match with the doctor,* she reasoned before rejecting the disloyal thought. No matter how afraid she had become of people, she couldn't begrudge potential happiness for her friend. Either Katie would remain her business partner or Melanie would have to figure something out. She had been managing to figure things out for years, she could keep right on doing so, she assured herself. With a firm twist she pushed the bolt into place to lock the door. It didn't seem likely that people barred their doors in these parts, but it would keep Melanie's mind more at ease, so it would be foolhardy not to do it.

ဆုဝဝ

Cole had watched the pretty woman walk away with very mixed feelings. He was a little shocked that she had left without a backward glance. He had thought they were having an enjoyable time together that morning working with the horse and then visiting with Leandra. But the woman was easy to spook. Worse than the horses, he thought irritably. She might be good looking, but he didn't need any further complications in his life, he reminded himself. Sheila was complicated, and look where that got him.

Glancing down at the puppy he still held in his arms, he smiled. The silly woman had seemed terrified of the small animal. Or perhaps not truly terrified of the pup, maybe she was terrified of having feelings for it. He could relate to that after the conversation they'd had that morning about Baby Foal.

He really ought to pick a name for the poor little thing. *What had she said for potential names?* he asked himself. She had some really intelligent suggestions. Who would have thought that the pretty face hid such a brilliant mind? He had enjoyed hearing her mention some Latin words. It had been so long since he had felt intellectually stimulated. Perhaps that would explain his unprecedented reaction to Miss Jones. He just wasn't used to talking to pretty women, or well-read people.

Feeling satisfied that he had reached the proper conclusion, he set those thoughts aside and turned his attention back to his daughter and her little friend. Miss Jones' gratitude for his keeping Annie had made him terribly uncomfortable. He should have been the one to be thanking her. Or rather Annie's mother, Mrs. Carter, he thought. With all the ranting Leandra had been doing lately, he was glad to be able to send Mary outside with a friend to play. The less she had to hear of her aunt's vitriol, the better. Cole sincerely hoped the visit with Miss Jones had done his sister enough good that she would lay off her angry ramblings for a while.

As he walked into the house, his hopes were dashed.

"This god forsaken place." She was clearly deep into a rant and hadn't required an audience to get started. Cole was both disappointed and relieved over the development. If she didn't need an audience, and the visit with Miss Jones this morning hadn't set her onto a saner path, it was obvious the poor dear must be actually ill, rather than just distempered. It helped him have greater sympathy for her, but also made him realize it was time to send her away. He couldn't have her around Mary in such a state.

After checking to make sure Leandra wasn't in danger of harming herself, he set off for the train station, composing the telegram in his head as he marched to the office. His heart ached over the thought of sending his sister away and reducing his family to the count of two. He hoped Mary would be all right without another female in the house. But being with just him was better than living with someone not of sound mind, he assured himself.

With a nod and a small coin, his message was sent. Someone from Boston would be on their way to collect her shortly. He was glad he had written to his family earlier to tell them this was a possibility. Cole would just have to keep his sister calm and safe for two more weeks at the most. Now to decide if it was best to tell her or not. While she had been raving about her hatred of Missouri for ages, she had always been free to leave. There was obviously something still holding her here. Cole worried that she might go a little madder if he told her she was to leave. He would have to broach the subject gently. Or maybe he could enlist help.

The rest of the day passed in a blur as he split his time between tending to his chores and checking on the girls. After the evening meal, Leandra had taken herself to her room so he didn't think he had to concern himself with her for the time being. It was a joy for him to see the wide grin splitting his daughter's face as she tumbled into bed with her little visitor. The two girls were asleep before their heads had even hit the pillow, it seemed. Cole could feel that his smile was a little melancholy as he gazed at the two little sleeping forms. His heart ached for both of them not having their mothers. But it didn't seem to weigh on either of their minds today as they had played at full speed all day and were now sleeping the sleep of the innocent.

Cole didn't begrudge them their innocent sleep, but he did envy them for it. He knew, despite the bone deep fatigue he was feeling, he wouldn't be able to reach the land of nod quite so easily. There were too many thoughts swirling through his mind. One of them was an idea his sister-in-law had planted there in her last letter. She had offered to help arrange a wife for him. The idea held merit. He truly did want a mother for Mary. But bringing yet another woman out here? Just the thought of it made his stomach ache. So far he had tried it twice, and neither time had worked out so well. Sheila, despite making the choice to marry him and knowing it would entail moving to Missouri, had struggled with settling in the West. And Leandra had hated Bucklin from the moment she had stepped foot off the train. At first, her devotion to Mary had helped her overcome her feelings about the western town, but her negative feelings had steadily increased despite her love for her family. Since Mary had started school, Leandra's decline had picked up speed. There was no way he could risk sending for another woman from the East. But there were so few single women available.

Punching his pillow into a more comfortable shape, Cole tried to arrange himself in the best position for sleep, but it continued to elude him.

He had heard there were other women who had arrived on the train. Other than Miss Jones, that was. While she was beautiful and intelligent, her anxious state didn't appeal to him. He had enough from his sister; he couldn't risk it in a wife. Marriage was forever, after all. Or until death. And he didn't wish to be widowed a second time. But Miss Jones' business partner was a widow, from what he understood. She might be worth making the acquaintance of. And since she had adopted Annie, she was obviously not averse to children, even other people's children, which boded well for his little Mary. Besides the fact that Mary and Annie were already close friends. It could almost be deemed meant to be. Of course, if there had already been one train load of children brought out from New York, there was a chance there would be more. And if this batch was escorted by single women, then maybe more would be on their way.

Rolling over again, Cole turned his mind to another idea. Maybe he ought to forget the idea of a mother for Mary. While Miss Jones seemed anxious and fidgety, she had been kind to the little girls. Maybe Cole could prevail upon her to take an interest in his daughter. All she really needed was a little bit of attention from an adult female, especially in a few years when she gets into the awkward phases of which he knew nothing. Maybe he should just ask about adopting some older boys to help him with the land. He didn't want Mary to be an only child, and he wanted someone to be able to leave his land to when the time came. He didn't want Mary to feel obliged to stay here, but a son would probably take to the work just like he had, he reasoned to himself.

Thus settled with a bit of a plan formed in his mind, Cole was finally able to drift into sleep. If it wasn't as restful as he had hoped, he didn't let it trouble him overmuch. He hopped out of bed at his usual time as soon as the cock began to crow at first light.

ℰᴑᴄℛ

Melanie was fidgeting. It was a telltale sign of her nerves, and she hated doing it, but it helped dispel the nervous energy. And there was no one around to take notice anyway. She had stopped by the Mitchells' house where Katie was stuck helping the doctor care for the deathly ill couple. Well, not so deathly ill after all, Melanie amended. Katie was fairly certain she would be able to return home that evening, and she hoped that Annie would be home when she got there. Melanie sighed. That meant she needed to be the one to go collect Annie. And explain to the child why her new mother wasn't at home waiting for her. Her stomach cramped just thinking about it. She started kneading a batch of bread in an attempt to dispel the anxiety.

Within a few hours, she had baked two dozen cookies, three loaves of bread, a pie, and was elbows deep in the preparations for a stew. Besides, all the sewing projects were completed. She had pretty much been in a frenzy. It was ridiculous. All because she didn't want to face the handsome rancher again, which was also ridiculous. Altogether, she, Melanie Jones, was ridiculous. If her dear mama were alive to see her now, she would surely be disappointed in her. Then again, if her dear mama were alive, she probably wouldn't have turned into a madwoman, she thought with a twist of her lips. Ah well, it must be borne. At least she had baked goods that she could take as a distraction for her sure-to-be-crazy behavior.

Katie would be pleased with how much of their work Melanie had managed to complete on her own. Maybe that would keep her from noticing that she had also depleted their flour supply, Melanie thought with a jolt of guilt. Good thing it wasn't overly expensive despite their isolated location. And with all the work she had done, surely they could afford some extra flour. Melanie began to fear that her circular thoughts really were a sign that she was losing her mind. She really ought to make a greater effort to not be so isolated. Perhaps she should have investigated whether the town offered religious services, since this was Sunday. But in the state of mind she had found herself after Katie asked her to collect Annie, it was doubtful she would have been welcomed in any congregation.

Melanie snorted at her own dark thoughts. *Now you really are being ridiculous, Miss Melanie,* she thought with a grin. *You might be a little off kilter, but surely no one could argue that anything you have said or done is completely beyond the pale. Now pull yourself together, go comb your hair, and head out to collect your friend's daughter. It shouldn't be so very challenging.*

Thus admonished, even if it was only by her own self, she set about righting her appearance and went on the prescribed errand. She dragged her feet a little as she neared the property, for which she again took herself to task. It really wouldn't do to be out after dark with Annie in tow. And it would be a long walk for the little girl, so she really ought to hurry. She brightened when she realized that could also be her excuse why she couldn't linger over collecting the youngster.

She had never walked so far during her days living in the city, but she was glad to observe that she was growing stronger each day. The long walk didn't even tire her anymore. And when she wasn't lagging with reluctance, her speeds were improving as well. While she had been thinking she and Katie should get a horse and wagon, she was glad to see that it wouldn't be a necessity, at least not for getting around the town. Of course, to visit anyone further afield, it would certainly come in handy. She certainly wouldn't want Katie to have to go much further afield than Mr. Miller's spread to visit any customers or to take Annie to play with friends.

Melanie could see the girls notice her from a distance. She had to bite her lip to hide her amusement as the two were clearly torn in their reactions to seeing her. The children were clearly pleased to see a familiar friendly face but also realized that Miss Jones' arrival spelled the end of their playtime together. Annie, still getting comfortable with her position within her household, didn't voice her disappointment, but her friend did enough complaining for the both of them.

"It's not even dark yet, Miss Jones, can't you stay a wee bit longer? Annie and I have been having too much fun for it to end yet."

"Mary, I'm sorry to disappoint you, but it would be best for us to get home before it gets dark. And surely you have things you'll need to get done in preparation for school tomorrow."

The little girl hung her head and scuffed her feet in disappointment. Melanie hated to sadden the children, so she quickly added, "I'm really happy to hear you had such a good time together.

We'll be sure to arrange for you to play together again soon. Maybe you can even come to stay over at our house some time soon."

"Really, Miss Jones? That would be grand." The little girls' exuberance made all three of them giggle. A fourth, deeper laugh joined in, startling Melanie.

"Good evening, Miss Jones. I see you've come to collect your charge. Would you like to come in for a cup of tea before you leave?"

Melanie made a show of glancing at the position of the sun before shaking her head. "Thank you for the offer, but I wouldn't want to get caught out in the dark, and I don't want Annie to have to run all the way home."

"We could hitch up the wagon and take you home," Mr. Miller offered.

Melanie was surprised at the chivalrous offer. "Surely that would be too much of an imposition."

"Not at all," he assured her, much to her consternation.

Feeling the hot color splashing up her cheeks, Melanie tried again to decline. "I wouldn't want you to have to put the horses to work on our behalf, and the walk will burn off the last of our energies so we'll sleep like logs tonight, right Annie?"

"I've never ridden in a wagon before," Annie answered, having no idea that Melanie was trying desperately to get away from the Millers.

Realizing it would be churlish to refuse further, Melanie accepted with as much good grace as she could manage. "Thank you for your continued kindness."

She was grateful that the task of hitching two horses to a wagon didn't take nearly as long as she would have expected. Before too many awkward minutes had passed, she was being handed up onto the seat, and the girls were clambering in behind. It was only when he was passing her Annie's small bag of belongings that Melanie realized she still held the parcel of cookies and bread she had brought for the Millers. Again her cheeks heated.

"How silly of me," she stammered. "I did some baking this afternoon and brought some for you."

Mr. Miller took an appreciative sniff. "I was hoping you were going to say that," he said with a grin, which only added to her discomfort as she realized he must have been able to smell the freshly baked items.

His chuckle at her embarrassment inexplicably settled some of her nerves, and she joined him in laughing. He took the small sack from her hands but placed it under his seat instead of putting it in the house before they left. "I don't want it to disappear before we get back," he explained with a wink that only made Melanie giggle a little more.

His humor had managed to set her at ease. The fact that they were sitting side by side instead of having to face one another also helped her discomfort. And the children's constant chatter filled the silence between them. The ruts in the road, though, caused their legs to bump together at times, and Melanie worried whether she ought to try to move away. She was grateful when he finally spoke, easing her sense of disquiet.

"Is everything well with Mrs. Carter?" he asked, keeping his voice quiet so Annie wouldn't hear.

"She expects to be home tonight or tomorrow at the latest. Since she dearly wishes to see Annie, she asked that she be brought home. It seems the worst of the illness has passed, and she won't be required any longer. And since Annie didn't succumb to the illness before, the doctor expects she won't this time either."

"It's a risk, though, bringing her home, isn't it?"

Melanie shrugged, biting her lip. "I sure hope not."

ஐ

Cole watched the woman bite her lip and had to bite his own to choke back his reaction. He fought the urge to bring his hand up and rub his thumb along the abused skin. He knew she would not welcome such familiarity. He feared she would even jump from the wagon, he thought with amusement. She was a flighty little female. He really ought not be so powerfully attracted to her. Perhaps it was merely the lack of female companionship. Just imagine how forward he would become after his sister had left. He averted his eyes to control his impulses.

"Do you not fear for yourself?" he asked, still keeping his voice low, hoping the girls didn't notice and think they were telling secrets.

"No." Her answer was abrupt. "I have been exposed to the illness, but I wasn't very sick when it swept through our building. I nursed many who died but for some reason, I was spared. I don't fear death, though, except for the sadness it would bring to my sister."

"That is rather macabre, isn't it, Miss Jones?"

She shrugged. "I don't search out death, Mr. Miller, but I've seen enough of it to think it more peaceful than life often is. But in this particular case, it would seem that Katie and I both have some level of immunity. As does Annie, for that matter. Her entire family died from the dread disease, and she didn't even get a sniffle, poor little soul."

He must have made a sympathetic noise of some sort because she finally turned her gaze his way and nodded as though in agreement with words unspoken.

"While family can be a trial, it is the source of all security when you are a child. I cannot bear to think on what the poor girl has gone through."

"You have a soft heart, Miss Jones," Cole commented begrudgingly.

His companion shrugged again. "I don't really think so. Anyone would feel sympathy for the poor lass, I would think. And it takes nothing from me to feel empathy for her. I know what it is to lose my mother, and I was ten. I cannot imagine losing everyone at half that age."

"My sweet girl lost her mother even earlier," he commented.

Her glance seemed to be filled with approval as she replied, "At least your daughter has a doting father. That must surely make up for some of the difference. You do realize how very rare such a devoted father is, don't you?"

Now it was Cole's turn to shrug. "She is my life. I will do anything for her."

There was a beat of silence while they both absorbed his words. He then continued, "Speaking of which, I have a favor to beg of you."

Her answering smile held a tinge of mischief despite the misgivings in her eyes. "It is only fair that favors be exchanged, I suppose."

"I do not mean it as a tit for tat, I assure you."

He was relieved to see her smile, but she still appeared wary.

"It is about Mary," he began, wishing he hadn't brought it up at this time but wondered when he would have another opportunity to speak with the timid woman. He could see that he had caught her attention and she was receptive to hear what he had to ask. "I have sent for someone to come for Leandra."

The expression on Miss Jones' face revealed that she recognized what a difficult decision that must have been, but she waited to comment until he had finished his explanation.

"I worry for Mary without a woman to answer certain questions for her," he explained as he felt heat rise in his cheeks again.

"Well, I think you're safe for a few years. The child is only five or six, after all."

"Yes, but for all my care of her, I still think girls need women in their lives. There is a shortage in Bucklin."

He felt her gaze searching his face and couldn't be sure what she saw there.

"Are you asking me to be a surrogate aunt to your daughter?" she asked, her voice gentle and understanding, which was remarkable considering her usual nervousness.

He was relieved. "Yes, that's it exactly."

She didn't accept immediately, which made him uncomfortable.

"I will have to explain to you one day why I hesitate, Mr. Miller. I can assure you it is not out of a disregard for your sweet daughter. And while I hesitate, I will not decline. I suppose if I can find it in my heart to allow Annie in, I can find room for Mary as well. Perhaps it will even be easier for there to be two rather than just one."

He didn't fully understand what she was saying, but contented himself that she had accepted. He reasoned that her obvious emotions would make her even more empathetic for Mary, and that was all he could ask for.

As they neared her small house with its neat little yard, he had to end the conversation lest the girls take note. "Thank you, Miss Jones, I will be forever in your debt." This brought a grin to her face.

"That sounds promising," she replied, causing him to laugh. For all her strangeness, he found her fascinating.

"You keep a tidy home, Miss Jones," he complimented as he helped her climb down from the wagon.

"Thank you," she answered, pride evident in her voice. "I cannot take all the credit, but both Katie and I are so happy about having a house to ourselves that we cannot cease puttering around and grooming it. The only thing we lack are flowers. I shall have to figure out how to move some from the field into our front yard. It would surely brighten up the place."

"I could probably help you with that. I have a shovel and some sacks."

Cole was amused to see her trying to get away from his offer. "Oh, no, Mr. Miller, I wouldn't want to trouble you in such a way. I'm quite certain Katie and I will be able to figure it out quite nicely on our own."

"So you find it promising for me to be in your debt, but have no wish for me to try to pay that off?"

Her face turned red, but she actually giggled as he handed her down from the wagon. "I think it is much better to keep the favor owing, just in case I ever truly have need of something."

Cole laughed. She was such a strange woman, mercurial and yet pleasant. He enjoyed her company despite her awkward ways. "You have an interesting philosophy, Miss Jones."

"Well, thank you for bringing us home. We'll now have a more comfortable evening." She was clearly dismissing him, and he was more disappointed than he should be. She looked down at the little girl by her side. "Do you have anything to say to Mr. Miller?"

His daughter's friend looked nervous but managed to look him in the face as she politely thanked him. "I had lots of fun. Thank you for letting me visit Mary and the puppies."

Cole leaned over and took the child's hand in a light shake. "It was our pleasure to have you, Annie. You are welcome to come over any time."

It was endearing how she grinned and turned her body from side to side in a display of bashfulness. The two adults exchanged amused glances.

"Goodnight, Mary, goodnight, Mr. Miller," Miss Jones called out in a sweet voice as she shepherded her young charge into the house.

Cole stood and watched until they were behind the closed front door. When he glanced over at his daughter who had remained in the wagon, she was looking at him with a questioning expression on her face. He grinned again. He was making a cake of himself; even his daughter thought so.

Darkness was falling as they neared home. "Did you enjoy having Annie around?"

"Oh yes, Papa, it was great fun. It's funny that there are so many things she's never done before, like playing with puppies, but she's game for trying. I like having someone to show things to. I wish Mama had gotten me a brother or sister before she died."

Cole blinked, unsure how to handle this unanswerable comment. "You don't think it might be annoying to have a younger brother or sister always under your feet?"

She shrugged. "Maybe a little bit, but it's probably better than always being by myself."

Cole's stomach clenched, and he fought a tide of fury at his dead wife. It was ridiculous to be angry with a dead woman. It's not as though she *meant* to die.

"Did you know Annie's 'dopted?" He was surprised by her turn of the subject.

"I did. Do you know what adopted means?"

"She said she lost her mama and papa and then got a new mama." She paused, obviously pondering the situation. "It's too bad she didn't get a new papa, too, but I s'pose it's better than not having anyone."

There was another pause while he could almost see her mind processing her thoughts.

"Maybe we should 'dopt someone, Papa."

He should have seen that coming, as he had thought it himself, but he was surprised that his daughter had arrived at that conclusion. Obviously, it wasn't something to take on lightly, but he decided to probe a little bit further.

"Would you prefer we adopt a brother or a sister for you?"

She responded with a serious face. "Maybe one of each would be a good idea. Or two boys and a girl so that we're even."

Now he couldn't hold back his chuckle. "You want to really expand our family now, don't you?"

She shrugged and then offered very mature logic for such a small girl. "The boys could help you with chores, and if I had a girl to help me, Aunt Leandra might be happier."

"Adding three extra people to our family might be a lot to get used to, though, don't you think?"

"Prob'ly. But it prob'ly would be lots of fun, too."

The grin that accompanied her words was infectious, and they arrived home in good humor. Cole had already made the arrangements for his sister to leave. He could see sense in his daughter's words about having help on the ranch. But taking responsibility for three additional children all at once was a little much for him to consider. Maybe he would ask Miss Jones the next time they crossed paths. She would know if was even feasible to consider. And she might have some words of wisdom as to things to consider. Thus settled, he was in a fine mood when he entered his home. But, it didn't last.

"Where have you been? I've been worried sick about you. It's late. Already dark. How could you leave me here by myself? Anything could have happened to me." Each word was louder and shriller than the one before. By the time Cole managed to step in and take control, Mary was in tears, and Leandra was wild eyed and wailing.

"Leandra, calm down." He wasn't sure if it was the best way to handle her, but he spoke with authority, which managed to cut through her hysteria and stemmed the flow of her words. "Nothing bad was going to happen to you. We weren't gone for very long. You were sleeping already when we left, so we thought we oughtn't disturb you, so we didn't tell you we were leaving. I'm sorry, we probably shouldn't have left you unannounced. But when Miss Jones arrived to collect Annie, Mary and I decided to give them a ride home so they wouldn't be out on their own in the dark."

"So, you were more concerned about the pretty stranger than about your own sister?" Leandra was turning mean in her anxious state.

Cole took a deep breath, trying to stay calm and collected. "Of course not, Leandra. You're my sister, and I care deeply about you. But you were safe here in the house. Those two would have been alone in the dark if we had allowed them to walk home. And little Annie was already tired after a long day of playing with our Mary. I thought it would be too much for them, and the neighborly thing was to give them a ride. What would you have had me do?" He was hoping to appeal to her logic.

"You should've told me they were here. You know I always want to have a visit with any women we might chance upon."

"Didn't you know that Mrs. Carter or Miss Jones would be coming to collect Annie?"

Apparently, she was done with his attempts at logic. She burst into tears. "You just don't understand," she bellowed before running into her room and slamming the door.

There was an eerie silence that followed the loud thud while Cole and Mary stood frozen in their places. Cole could barely bring himself to look at his daughter. He should have contacted his family weeks ago. He would have never wanted his child to witness a scene such as this.

"I guess we shoulda told her," Mary said, a shrug in her voice, as though her aunt's explosion were a thing of little note.

Cole grinned. "I guess so." He paused for a moment, waiting to see if Mary would have any further reaction. When she just smiled at him, he blinked before changing the subject. "Off to bed with you, little miss. You have to be wide awake for school tomorrow."

"All right, Papa." She skipped away as though she hadn't a care in the world.

Cole was disconcerted. He was glad Mary didn't seem to be overly disturbed by the scene with Leandra, but he didn't like that his sister's outbursts were so commonplace to his daughter that she had little or no reaction. He certainly didn't want her thinking such outbursts were acceptable behavior. But how to discuss it? Perhaps he could ask Miss Jones. He didn't want to become dependent on that strange woman, either, though. He ought to be able to raise his daughter on his own. But he had already asked her for her assistance, and she had agreed, so maybe it wouldn't be so very strange to discuss this with her.

Chapter Seven

K atie was finally home and settling back into the fabric of their lives, except that her mind wasn't really there. It was obvious that at least half the time her thoughts were elsewhere while a silly smile stretched her face.

Melanie was happy for her friend, *truly she was*, she insisted to herself. She didn't want to think that she was such a curmudgeon that she would begrudge her friend some happiness. But she dreaded the change that was clearly on the horizon. They had barely gotten settled here in the small town of Bucklin. But they were doing well, had clients building up, and their little house was clean and well cared for. Melanie wanted to be happy, content with the way things were. But she doubted they were going to stay this way much longer, and for that she was a bundle of nerves.

Of course, with Katie all aflutter over the doctor, much of Annie's care was falling to Melanie. Not to say that Katie was neglecting her daughter. She was very much involved in her every day activities, but there were frequent occasions when Katie was off with the doctor, and Melanie was left to keep the child entertained.

Annie was a sweet, friendly little girl, so Melanie didn't mind it terribly, but she couldn't decide how to feel about Katie and Dr. Jeffries, which made it difficult to deal with the child's persistent questions about them.

"Do you like Dr. Jeffries, Melanie?" was today's awkward question as they were stirring cookie dough together in the small kitchen.

Melanie bit her lip. "He seems like a kind gentleman," she answered as diplomatically as she could. "How do you feel about him?"

The little girl didn't answer for some time. "Well, I don't like doctors."

"I can understand that. You haven't had much good experience with them, have you?"

Annie shook her head vigorously.

"But doctors are supposed to help people, aren't they?"

"I s'pose."

"So that's a good thing, wouldn't you say?"

Annie shrugged, not wanting to admit to such a thing.

With a smile she tried to suppress, Melanie persisted. "Have you ever had an uncomfortable experience with Doctor Jeffries?"

"What do you mean?"

"Has he ever made you angry or sad or upset?"

"Well, only because I don't like doctors."

Now Melanie couldn't hold back her laughter. "I understand that part, but what about Dr. Jeffries specifically? Has he ever been mean to you?"

"He was mean to Mama Kate. Remember when I jumped out of Suzie's barn?"

Melanie nodded. "That was a scary time, wasn't it?" The child nodded, too. "Why do you suppose the doctor was mean to Katie?"

"He thinks every little girl should have a mama and a papa and that my mama works too hard."

"There's nothing wrong with that, is there? It would be better to have both, if it can be managed, don't you think?"

Annie looked at her with wise eyes. "I like it how things are just fine."

Melanie smiled. "Well, it seems that Doctor Jeffries has gotten over his thoughts about your mama, so maybe you should try to get over your thoughts about him."

Annie scrunched her nose as she considered Melanie's words. "Well, he does bring me lemon drops from the mercantile whenever he calls round."

With a laugh, Melanie said, "There you go — he's clearly not all bad, is he?"

The little girl still looked skeptical, so Melanie thought she ought to try a little harder. "It seems to me that your mama is quite happy when she comes home from her walks with the doctor. Have you noticed that?"

"She sings or hums. Is that what you mean?"

"Yes, those are signs that she's happy."

"I want her to be happy." The child's tone was grudging and hesitant. Melanie decided it was enough for the time being.

"Of course, you do. And I want you to be happy. So, what would make you happy this afternoon?"

"Are you finished with your work for today?"

Melanie hated that the little girl was still so guarded. It was unfortunate that her mother was bringing change when the poor child was still so unsettled after the recent adoption. But these things couldn't be helped, she supposed.

"I am quite finished. Once our cookies are done, I have nothing left to do except spend time with you."

Annie clapped her hands and did a wiggling little dance. "Do you s'pose Mr. Miller would mind if we came to look at the puppies?"

Melanie's stomach dropped in dismay. She had managed to avoid the subject of Mr. Miller for more than a week. It had been causing her a little bit of discomfort, as she had promised the man to show an interest in his daughter. But the unsettled feelings he stirred in her were more than she wanted to face. With a sigh, Melanie answered.

"I doubt if he would begrudge us the fun. Have you been speaking with Mary at school? Has she told you anything about the pups?"

"She said they grow overnight and are getting to be even more squirmy."

"That sounds like fun, doesn't it?"

Annie's vigorous nodding convinced Melanie that she would just have to gird her loins mentally and face the man. He wasn't so terrible, she reminded herself as she bustled about, tidying the small house and herself before setting out on the long walk.

"Should we take a few cookies for the Millers?"

"For sure," came Annie's quick reply.

"What about something for us? Are we likely to get hungry on the way? Do you want me to bring an apple for you to munch on later?"

"Thank you, Melanie. And bring one for you, too."

Melanie smiled over the little girl's polite thoughtfulness. It was a shame she had faced such tragedy in her young life, but it had obviously forged her into a pleasant little person. Melanie chuckled as she arranged the cookies and a couple apples in a small sack to be comfortably carried on their trek.

She marveled over Annie's energy as the little girl bounded around her as they made their way to the Miller's ranch. Melanie thought she should admonish her not to expend so much energy before they even got there but thought better of it. The sweet child was so biddable, she would do as she was told, but Melanie hesitated to suppress her exuberance. Melanie just didn't want to have to carry her home if she exhausted herself completely. So, she let the child continue her chatter and energetic play.

The fence posts marking the turn onto the Miller property were well behind them by the time they finally caught sight of the house and barn. Melanie was surprised once more by how large the property was. Mr. Miller had mentioned on their first visit that it spread out behind for at least a mile. She hadn't thought to ask how far it went in the other directions. But it was large. And she was tired from the walk. She had thought she was getting accustomed to walking, but she probably ought to walk more on a regular basis. Perhaps it wouldn't seem so very far if she were more used to it. Not that she needed to get used to walking to the Miller place, she admonished herself.

Someone on the property must have spotted them because Mary came bounding out of the house, excited to see them before they even reached the porch.

"I'm so happy to see you! Can you stay for supper?"

Melanie blinked. "Oh no, we wouldn't want to impose. We were just wondering if we could see the puppies again."

"Of course!" Mary exclaimed. "But you should stay for supper, too."

Melanie laughed. "That's kind of you to offer, Mary, thank you. We could maybe have a cup of tea with you, but we should get along home before supper. Annie's mother doesn't know we've come, and we wouldn't want to make her worry."

Melanie couldn't interpret the look that crossed the child's face, but Mary quickly agreed. "No, you definitely wouldn't want her to worry. Let me just ring the bell so Papa knows you've come, and then we can go in the barn."

"Oh, we needn't disturb your father," Melanie quickly interjected. "He's surely busy with important things."

"I think he'd be happy to have a visitor," the child insisted as she banged on the loud bell and the sound rang out in an almost deafening manner.

"Well, no one could miss that," Melanie commented, her tone dry.

Mary grinned.

"Is your aunt up for visitors?" Melanie thought to ask.

"She's lying down," Mary answered with a guilty face. "I prob'ly shouldn't have rang the bell quite so good."

Melanie laughed. "Well, she was happy to have a visitor the last time I was here, so she probably won't mind if you woke her up."

The child looked doubtful but wasn't allowed to dwell on it overly. Annie's impatience to see the pups couldn't be quelled.

"Can we go to see them now, please? I promise I cannot wait another minute." She was hopping from foot to foot in a manner that made all three of them break into giggles. Mary led the way to the barn.

They were so engrossed in the small animals that Melanie barely registered his presence until Mr. Miller spoke at her shoulder.

"Good afternoon. It's a pleasant surprise to see you two."

Stifling her gasp of surprise, Melanie turned to him with a smile. "Good afternoon. I hope we haven't disturbed you too much. Mary insisted you would want to know we're here. Annie wanted to see the puppies again."

"And so you walked all the way here?" He was incredulous.

"It's not so very far." Melanie was embarrassed, but Annie hadn't even noticed Mr. Miller's arrival.

He must have realized he was making her uncomfortable, as he quickly tried to change the subject.

"Mary was quite correct. I would be very disappointed to find out we had visitors and I hadn't been called to say hello. Do say you'll stay for tea."

Despite her discomfort, Melanie agreed. "Mary actually invited us to stay for supper, but we had to explain that Mrs. Carter didn't know we were here so we couldn't do that. But tea would be lovely, thank you."

He too got a strange look on his face when she said Katie didn't know where they were. "Did Mary say anything when you said that?"

"No, but her face looked sort of like yours does now. What have I said that's so wrong?"

He quickly shook his head. "It isn't you. It's what you said." Her face must have given away that he wasn't making it better because he quickly recovered with, "That is to say, what you said reminded us of something that happened with Leandra a week ago."

"Oh dear, something not good, from the looks of your faces."

"When we got home from driving you and Annie home, she was a little put out that we hadn't told her we were going."

"Oh no, I thought she was sleeping when we left."

"She was. But she woke up."

"Is she afraid of being by herself?"

"It would seem so. It had never been a problem before, that I knew of, but then it might not have ever happened before."

"Poor thing. I'm sorry that we were inadvertently the cause of trouble."

"Don't be. It is absolutely not your fault. And how were any of us to know she would wake up and be nervous?"

ℴ)Ↄ

The humming sound she made low in her throat let him know Melanie didn't exactly accept his absolution. She looked worried, as though she were wishing she hadn't come to visit. Even though she was always so strange and awkward, he liked having her there. He needed to set her back at ease.

"By the way, thanks for your help in naming the horse. A new foal just arrived yesterday, so Gem got her name just in time."

"You went with Gem!" A wide smile split her face. "That's great. She must be happy to have a real name now."

Cole tried not to look so skeptical as he said, "I'm not sure if she really noticed. She certainly didn't take it personally."

Miss Jones' warm chuckle tickled his ears. "You never know. I think animals might be more intuitive than you think. But in either case, it would have been far too confusing to have two Baby Foals on the property."

"That is certainly true."

He watched as she bent down and picked up one of the puppies, who was making a beeline to the end of the stall. "You're a little adventurer, aren't you, my furry friend." When she turned to face him, her eyes were full of warmth. "This one is going to be trouble, I'm afraid. He doesn't seem inclined to remain with his siblings."

"A sense of adventure might serve him well when he's big enough to train. It means he won't be timid or easily intimidated by the animals he's supposed to be shepherding."

Her warm gaze was full of curiosity. "Do you train them yourself? Have you done it often?"

He wanted to tug his collar. "Well, I trained his mother. I've trained a couple others and traded them for services."

Her cocked head indicated she wanted to learn more. "It didn't seem right to charge someone for a dog, even if he was well trained. So, I gave a couple of the trained pups away in exchange for help building my fence, for one, and I got a new ram for another."

"That seems to be a smart way of doing things," she observed. Her admiring tone made his chest feel like it was puffing up with pride. "Do you have similar plans for these puppies?"

His glance found his daughter and her friend with puppies in each of their laps. He had to laugh softly. "I have a feeling it will be a little bit harder this time. We haven't had puppies with her old enough to remember."

Melanie again made that rumbling sound in her throat, but this time it seemed to him to be sympathetic. "Maybe keeping one might help with various transitions you all will be facing soon."

Cole's throat tightened. Having an empathetic, intelligent adult to share life's burdens with was something he had been sorely missing. Maybe he should take his sister-in-law up on her offer of sending him a wife. But he just couldn't take the risk. He had already been down this road twice to pain and suffering all around. He surely wished some of his family would come for a visit, but they had wired to say that an official from a hospital would be coming to collect Leandra. He suspected it was going to be trouble. He cleared his throat.

"Could I please ask your advice on something, Miss Jones?"

She chuckled softly. "You can certainly ask, but I cannot guarantee that I'll have anything useful to offer."

He grinned in response. "That's fair enough. My family has wired to say that rather than come themselves to collect Leandra, they are sending someone from a hospital they want her to go to."

"Oh dear, that's unfortunate, isn't it?"

"Yes, I don't actually think she's so far gone that she needs to go into a place like that. But sending a stranger for her might make her worse, and then she'll need it. I feel so guilty."

"I can understand why you might feel that way, but in my opinion, you ought not to do so. You made the decision to contact your family, both for your daughter's and your sister's welfare. It is a little less than ideal that they decided to handle it in this way, but they're her family, too. Maybe there are factors you don't know anything about. And maybe it'll be for the best this way."

"I hope you're right." He hated sounding so fearful to his own ears and couldn't quite meet her gaze due to his embarrassment.

When she reached out and put her hand on his arm, he almost jumped with surprise, but the warm pressure of her small hand felt so good he wondered how he could prolong the sensation. It seemed to be exactly what he needed in that moment. But then it appeared as though she thought better of the impulse and pulled her hand back, quickly gripping it with her other hand. Her face took on that scrunched up, nervous appearance that he hated to see, as though she were afraid of whatever was coming next.

She cleared her throat, a delicate but nervous sound. "We really ought to be going. We just wanted to venture over for a few minutes of playing with the puppies. Annie and I don't want to intrude on you and your family."

It looked as though she were going to run out on them. "Have you changed your mind about staying for a cup of tea?"

Her face flamed with color, and she started to stammer. "Well, no, I, uh, just don't want to intrude on your family situation."

"It's no intrusion. I promise you. If Leandra is awake, I'm sure she'll be happy to see you. If she's not, Mary and I will enjoy your company."

Her high color didn't recede noticeably, but she didn't decline either, busying herself with collecting the puppy who was again trying to escape the confines of the stall. When she briefly cuddled the little animal tenderly to her chest, Cole felt his own chest constrict. It was such an unconscious action, as though she couldn't help herself. He was shocked to realize that he was jealous of the pup.

He too cleared his throat of discomfort. "I'll just go put the kettle on the stove to boil. Come in when you're ready."

Miss Jones cast him a half smile as she kept her face partially averted. He thought the little girls hadn't even noticed his words, but then his daughter called out.

"Thank you, Papa, we'll be right there." There was a muffled protest from what must have been Annie before Cole heard his daughter explaining, "But Annie, I can barely wait to eat some of those cookies you brought." This was followed by at least two females giggling, so Cole was left to surmise that Annie wasn't begrudging his daughter her tea. He hurried away to do as he had said.

Chapter Eight

Melanie was nervous. She rubbed her hands briskly against her skirt as she walked with the girls back to the house. She wished she had worn gloves, but she realized that would have been ridiculous in this heat and location. The Millers would have thought her pretentious, she was sure, putting on airs like some debutante from the Upper Side of New York. Her friend, Cassandra, who *was* a debutante, could have certainly pulled it off with aplomb, but Melanie was certain she would have just looked ridiculous. Of course, most all women wore gloves on formal occasions, even out here in Bucklin. She had noticed some of the women in the mercantile had worn gloves. But she would have looked absurd walking out to visit puppies with her gloves on. And her only owning one good pair anymore. The adorable little animals would have greatly enjoyed ripping them to shreds.

Sighing, Melanie tried to bring her thoughts into order. *Mr. Miller is merely being neighborly by offering us tea. Anyone would do the same thing,* she reminded herself. *I would make the same offer if the roles were reversed,* she insisted. Besides, *he wants help calming his sister, to be sure, the poor dear.*

Who's going to look after me so kindly when I go stark, raving mad? Melanie asked herself, her stomach clenching as she tried to shove the unwelcome thought away. *Who says you haven't already?* she mocked herself. This last thought caused her lips to tip up in genuine amusement. It was at that moment that her gaze was ensnared by that of Mr. Miller, and the pit of her stomach dropped down for a moment.

I wonder if this is what Katie is always talking about when she speaks of the doctor. She says she gets butterflies in her tummy. That sounds pleasant enough. Not like this queasy feeling I have when my heart is racing and I think I might be ill. Gulping for air, Melanie tried to still her racing thoughts. *It's just tea! Everyone drinks tea. The little girls are present. And oh look, there's Leandra. Oh dear, she doesn't look well.*

"Miss Jones," Leandra said, her voice hoarse.

"Please, you must call me Melanie as we agreed last time."

"Oh yes, pray excuse me. I had quite forgotten." Melanie didn't think she had, as her tone wasn't in the least genuine, but she allowed the statement to pass without argument.

"Your voice sounds a bit strained, Leandra. Have you been unwell?"

"In a manner of speaking," Leandra replied while her gaze darted around as though she couldn't settle on anything.

Melanie was confused until it dawned on her that perhaps the poor woman had been yelling herself hoarse. Her eyes sought out Mr. Miller's gaze. He looked resigned, and Melanie felt stricken. What tragedy.

Melanie thought a change of topic was in order. "Annie and I made some extra cookies this afternoon and thought we would bring them by and get a peek at the puppies." Leandra didn't make any comment in return so Melanie kept on. "It's hard not to lose your heart to the dear little animals, isn't it?"

When Leandra still didn't say anything, Melanie gave up and turned to Mary to ask, "Are dogs your favorite animal, Mary?"

The little girl scrunched up her face while she thought about her answer. "I love the puppies and really all dogs, but I think my favorite animal is a bobcat."

"A bobcat? Well, that's not at all the answer I was expecting. Is there a reason why a bobcat is your favorite?"

"They eat rats," the little girl answered simply. "I really don't like rats. I don't mind mice, but rats are too big for my liking."

"I can't say that I blame you for that." Melanie tried not to shudder as she thought of her next question. "Are there many rats around?"

"They like to eat the horse feed."

"Oh dear. Do the horses mind?" Melanie lamented her limited knowledge of animals and wildlife.

Mary shrugged. "I don't know if they mind sharing their food, but they don't like rats either. Some of the horses are afraid of them."

"I can understand that," Melanie answered with a nervous giggle. "I think I agree with you that bobcats are pretty great if they keep the rats under control. But aren't bobcats a little scary?"

"No, they're more scaredy than scary," Mary answered with a wide smile. "I wish they weren't so scaredy. They look pretty soft. I would like to pet one someday."

Melanie bit her lip and glanced at the child's father. He met her gaze and rolled his eyes. Seeing the humor lurking in their depths made Melanie need to fight not to burst into more giggles. Melanie turned back to the children.

"What about you Annie? Do you have a favorite animal?"

"I love the puppies. I wish we could have one. Or maybe a kitten. But I think I love most the birds that sing outside my window every morning. It's the happiest sound I ever heard. It's so much better than what we heard before."

Melanie glanced at her small companion and was forced back to her last morning in New York. Once again, she had been awakened by the shrewish yelling of the woman who lived across the hall as her husband left for work.

"You better not be late coming home for supper again tonight, Murray. I won't be cooking your meals any longer if you leave them to congeal on the stove."

Who would want to come home to that welcoming screech? she thought as she rolled over and punched her pillow, trying to find a soft spot for her head.

But sleep would not be returning to her. Murray's departure had set the building in motion, and everyone was stirring. She had left the window open the night before in an effort to air out their rooms. The air was fresher, but through the opening could be heard the sound of horse shoes on cobblestones as the deliveries were being made up and down the street.

Then there was the heavy clomp of someone going back up the stairs carrying their family's water. Melanie needed to bestir herself and do the same. It was the last time she would have to do it, she reminded herself with a grin. While she was certain there would be effort required in fetching water in Missouri, she was determined that she would never again live on the fourth floor of a five-storey building. The heat and the odors always rose unpleasantly, especially in the summer.

And having to go all the way down to the courtyard to relieve nature or fetch water was not something she wanted to continue doing for the rest of her life.

Blinking the vivid memory away, Melanie smiled at Annie. "I think I will agree with you, my dear. I love that cheerful sound in the morning, too. We should find out if that particular bird has a name so we can be certain of what our favorite is called."

Annie grinned back at her, pleased with the adult's reaction.

"I have a favorite," Mr. Miller interjected, gaining him all the females' attention.

Melanie smiled when she noticed his cheeks coloring. She prompted him. "What is it?"

"The red fox, even though he will eat the chicks if I'm not careful."

Melanie was surprised. "Why would he be your favorite if he might eat some of your animals?"

"I think I'm like my daughter — I just want to pet him." He chuckled softly. "Have you ever seen a fox up close?" When both Melanie and Annie shook their heads vigorously, he elaborated. "Their red coat looks so thick and soft, I would love to sink my fingers into it and then scratch him behind the ears. And then there's the fact of how smart they seem to be. Wiley, you might say. The length I've had to go to keep the chicks safe, gives me a certain level of respect for the sneaky little creatures."

All the girls laughed along with him, except Leandra who was glowering by herself, silently observing them as they conversed. Finally, Melanie had reached the end of her tolerance and stood to take their leave.

"It was pleasant visiting with the three of you for a few minutes. Thank you for the tea and for allowing us a bit of time with the puppies. Annie and I ought to be on our way. We shall see you again soon, to be sure."

Melanie could see the understanding shining in Mr. Miller's eyes, and she almost faltered in her determination to leave. She felt terrible about leaving him to deal with his situation on his own, but she reminded herself that it *was* his situation to deal with. Perhaps he wasn't even looking for her help or sympathy, she reminded herself. He was just a kind man who had a terrible circumstance to deal with, and he understood that she didn't want to deal with it. There was nothing so terrible in that, was there? She kept her face as neutral as possible as she herded Annie from the room while saying their goodbyes.

On the walk home, she was glad that Annie was so energetically occupying herself because Melanie wasn't going to be of much company. Her mind had remained behind at the Millers' place. She thought back to the terrible situation she had lived through herself. Becoming the woman of the house at the age of ten had been more than she could handle, but she had managed. Her sister and brother were healthy and reasonably happy. For that she was grateful. The blame for the fact that she had become so fearful of everything rested solely on her own shoulders. She shouldn't have allowed it to come to this, but she was proud of herself for braving the huge change of leaving New York and moving to Missouri.

She had never told Katie the details of her situation and that sweet woman, having issues of her own to cope with, had never pressed her, merely picking up the slack of what she could or could not handle. Melanie would walk through fire for her friend. And at times, taking her friend's daughter out in public felt like walking through fire, but she was managing, and she was quite sure she wasn't projecting her issues onto Annie, which was her deepest fear. That poor child would have her own emotional baggage to live with given her background; she didn't need Melanie's issues besides.

"Miss Melanie?"

"Yes, my dearest Annie?"

"Do you think Mama Kate will have a baby if she marries the doctor?"

Melanie's heart sank. She didn't want to be the one to talk to Annie about her mother's potential marriage or the consequences of what that marriage might mean for Annie. But there was no one else about, and the child needed to be answered.

"It's quite possible. Do you think you would like a little brother or sister?"

Annie wrinkled her nose as she pondered the question. "I think it would be lovely to have brothers and sisters again. But maybe Mama Kate would love a baby more than me."

Melanie had wondered if that's where this conversation was leading. But she couldn't let the moment pass. She stopped in her tracks and knelt down in front of Annie, not heeding the dirt and what it might do to her skirts. Taking the little girl's hands firmly into her grasp, she looked Annie in the eye and reassured her.

"Your mama loves you from the very bottom of her heart. Nothing will ever change that. Not even if she has ten babies. I promise you, truly. Your mother is loyal and true. And she has enough love in her heart and soul for many children."

The little girl looked somewhat mollified by Melanie's words but not completely reassured, so Melanie continued questioning the child's reasons for asking.

"Are you worried about the fact that you're adopted?"

Annie nodded vigorously. "She hasn't known me all my life."

"Do you really think that matters?" Melanie wanted to understand where the child was coming from.

"I don't know." Annie's answer was glum.

"Has anyone said something to you to make you think like this?"

The guilt on the child's face made Melanie's heart sink.

"Was it at school?" She kept her voice gentle even though she wanted to smack someone. How could children be so cruel?

Annie's nod was almost imperceptible. Melanie struggled to reassure the child.

"Do you truly believe your mama loves you?"

Annie shrugged but gave a small nod. Melanie couldn't really fault the poor girl; she had been through a lot in her young life.

"I truly believe she does," Melanie assured her. "I think you should try to talk to her about this. I know for sure she wouldn't want you to be afraid to talk to her about anything. And you know what? It's not even for sure that she'll marry the doctor, anyway."

The hopeful look on the little girl's face made Melanie's stomach hurt. She didn't want to encourage Annie to think the couple might not last, so she changed the subject slightly.

"When a mama has a new baby, the baby needs a lot of attention at first. You probably realize that, right?" Annie's puzzled face made her explain further. "Remember the first time we saw the puppies?" This brought a grin to Annie's solemn face. "What did you notice about them?"

"They were really little."

"Right. What else? Could they move very fast or look after themselves?"

Vigorous head shaking followed this. "No, they could only crawl over each other, and they were all trying to get to their mama so they could eat."

"Exactly. And human babies can't even crawl when they're born. It takes them months before they can. So, the human mother has to do everything for the baby. Just like puppies, human babies are really cute, and the mother loves them, so she does everything for the baby. But they aren't really all that interesting. Even though mamas sing to their babies and even talk to them, they can't have a conversation like you and I are having. So, if your mama has more babies in the future, she'll still love you and want you around. You could be a really big help for her if there are babies, you know."

Not that Melanie really wished that on the little girl, but she knew it was the natural way of things. And she was sure the poor child wouldn't be put in the same position Melanie had been when her mother died after giving birth to her little brother. Melanie was completely sure that Katie would be able to balance a baby with showing attention to her growing daughter.

"That might be fun." The child sounded uncertain, but at least she was willing to see a better side to the possibilities.

"Since there's no use worrying about it at this point, since your mama has only just started courting with the doctor so any babies are still a long way off, let us turn our minds to something much more interesting," Melanie declared in as droll a voice as she could manage.

It did the trick. The little girl burst into giggles.

"Like what?" Annie asked between her laughter.

"Well, I don't know about you, but I'm starving! Are you even a teensy bit hungry?"

Vigorous nodding was the only answer she got as the little girl was still dissolving in laughter.

"I think we should have mashed potatoes and fried eggs for supper. What do you think?"

"Sounds delicious."

"And maybe some of the bread and cookies we made earlier would go well with it."

"M'hmm."

They continued the rest of the way home, skipping and laughing. But Melanie was troubled and determined to speak to her friend about her child's concerns.

Chapter Nine

"Oh Melanie, I'm sorry that you had to deal with that." Katie was stricken.

"I'm not telling you to make you feel badly, Kate, I promise you."

"No, of course not, but I do none the less."

Melanie couldn't help smiling over her words, not over the situation. "I guess I can understand why. But while I do think you need to have a conversation with Annie about your possible future, I don't think she's as troubled now as she was before she and I talked." They were silent for a moment before Melanie continued. "My biggest concern is what the other children seem to be saying to her. I was too busy reassuring her of her place in your heart that I forgot to get more details about what some little monster might have said to her."

Katie chuckled over her friend's words. "I don't think the children are monsters."

"Well I do, if they're going to make our Annie feel unsettled," Melanie interrupted, causing Katie to laugh some more.

"While I'm delighted that you are taking your role as honorary aunt to my daughter so seriously. You have to watch that you don't become too ferocious in your protective stance. Perhaps she misunderstood or jumped to conclusions based on some other child's fears. You never know, maybe one of the other children has a new baby brother or sister and is feeling misplaced. One thing could lead to another. You know how children's minds jump to the most convoluted places sometimes."

Melanie had to force herself to see what Katie was saying. "I guess you're right. But I can empathize with Annie's fears, and it might've made me a little overprotective."

"Maybe a little," Katie agreed with a dry tone, making Melanie finally join in the laughter.

"Oh very well, I am a she-bear when it comes to the children in my care. That is as it should be. But never mind about that for now. I've told you, now it's your responsibility. But nothing can be done about it now, so you absolutely must tell me all about your excursion with the good doctor. I still cannot believe how quickly you have made an about face from loathing the man to being all starry eyed about him."

Melanie felt a stab of envy as her friend's smile turned secretive, even though Katie laughed at her words. "I wouldn't say I loathed the man."

At Melanie's raised eyebrow Katie giggled. "Well, all right, the relationship was pretty cold at first. But as you can see, these things can change pretty quickly, so you better watch out for yourself. With how outnumbered women are to men in this town, it could happen to you, even if you don't think you're susceptible. Look at me! I swore up and down I would never even consider remarriage, and now here I am courting with the doctor!" She seemed momentarily shocked by the thought before drifting off into dreamy reminiscence. "We did have a lovely afternoon yesterday. We walked up to the point again where he asked me to court. It is the most lovely view. And we talked and talked. As you know, the time got away on us."

Melanie laughed. "Yes, I know. You got in just in time to say goodnight to Annie."

"Am I abusing your friendship completely? I know you didn't sign up for mothering duties."

"No, no, I'm not filling mothering duties. I am strictly the favorite aunt. And I make no promises about not spoiling your child. It'll be left to you to unravel whatever messes I might make with the girl."

Katie laughed. "I trust you implicitly."

There was a pause while Melanie pondered her words. Always perceptive, Katie prodded. "Something else is on your mind. You made a weird face when I said that I trust you. Do you not think I should?"

Melanie's laugh sounded forced as she responded. "No, it's not that. Of course, I think you should trust me. I will guard Annie with my life. And I was only joking when I said that I'll spoil her. In your absence, I will do the best I possibly can."

"I know, thus the implicit trust. So, spit it out. Something is bothering you."

Melanie sighed and decided to confide in her friend. "Mr. Miller has asked me to take an interest in Mary."

Katie frowned. "Annie's friend? Why would he do that? Doesn't he have a wife?"

"No, that's what I thought, too, but it's his sister. And she's not well. Please don't share this with any of our clients, but he has contacted his family back East and asked them to come for her. Apparently, she hates it here in Bucklin and has only been staying from a sense of duty toward her brother and niece. Now that Mary is going to school, Mr. Miller feels that he can manage without her, and perhaps they will be better off without her negative presence."

Katie's eyebrows had been steadily rising throughout Melanie's explanation. "He has certainly confided a fair bit of information to you."

Melanie could feel heat rising in her face, and she began to feel defensive. "I think he felt he had nowhere to turn and was hoping for a female perspective."

Katie's eyebrows remained elevated. "So, he confided in a woman he just met rather than one of his neighbors that he's known for years? Ones who perhaps have even known his sister?"

Melanie frowned. "Do you think it's worrisome that he has discussed this with me? I think he just thought that since I am spending time with Annie, I might be in a position to take an interest in Mary and spend some time with her, too."

Katie's face split into a grin. "I don't think it's worrisome at all. But I think it is exactly what I was talking about. I've seen Mr. Miller. He is a handsome man. And from the gossip I've picked up around town while visiting our clients, it would seem he is quite well-to-do."

"His lands certainly seem to be extensive. But why does that make you look so strangely all of a sudden?"

"You are a good looking, intelligent, single woman. If a good looking, intelligent, single gentleman starts confiding in you, it could only mean one thing. I won't be the only one courting before long."

"No. Absolutely not. He is not interested in me in that way. He is merely concerned for his daughter. And he did us a favor, if you will recall, when you were stuck at the Mitchells' house with their illness. He kept Annie for us and prevented her from even realizing that you were gone until it was all over. We owe him our kindness for what he did."

"Why are you protesting so much? Are you really that opposed to a man showing a romantic interest in you?"

"He hasn't shown a romantic interest in me, Katie. I'm not like you. You're pretty and witty and energetic and outgoing. And you're such a tiny little woman. I think men like that. I'm awkward and nervous and shy and clumsy. I don't know what to say to people, and I would far rather stay at home than go out into the world. Surely, someone like Mr. Miller would prefer anyone else over me."

Loyal Katie swept to her defense. "For one thing, you are the loveliest friend I've ever had. I think you're beautiful. In the sunlight, your brown hair is every shade of nutmeg and walnut and amber."

Melanie laughed. "You make me sound like a tree."

Not to be deterred, Katie persisted. "And you're so smart. When you aren't nervous, you have the most fascinating things to talk about."

"But I'm always nervous," Melanie complained. "But never mind. I don't even want him to be interested in me, so it doesn't matter. I mean, really, what would I do with a man? He will want more children, and I don't know if I could bear it. I've already raised my family."

Katie's laughing face softened into concern. "But a family of your very own is different than your siblings. And having a husband would be a completely different scenario than an absent father who only makes demands of you."

"I'm sure it is, but I have no interest in learning it for myself, so never mind about it. I'm just glad to see you so happy."

"Now you're just trying to change the subject," Katie laughed. "But what are you going to do about Mary?"

Melanie sighed. "I don't know. The poor dear thing. I was thinking of offering to have her come stay with us for a few days when her aunt is being taken away. It's sure to be an ugly scene that no little girl should witness. Would you be accepting of having her with us?"

"Of course," was Katie's immediate reply. "Do you think we should go see if we can help the poor woman?"

"Maybe you should go. You're so much better with people than I am," Melanie protested.

"But I have barely met her, just in passing at the school. I think it would be much more comfortable for everyone if you came with me." Now Katie had begun wheedling.

"Not more comfortable for me," Melanie pointed out with a weak laugh.

"Come on, it's time for you to get out of the house."

"I was just out of the house yesterday. Remember the uncomfortable conversation I had with your daughter on the way to that very house?"

"Bringing up my guilt over Annie isn't going to help you get out of coming with me," Katie answered tartly, but her laugh gave away that she held no hard feelings. "Come along, you can make your offer to Mr. Miller while the children aren't there to overhear and pressure him into it if he doesn't think it's the right choice."

With a sigh, Melanie capitulated. "Very well, just let me wash my face and tidy my hair. It wouldn't do for any potential clients seeing me a mess," she explained when she caught sight of Katie's arched brows.

"M'hmm," Katie hummed. "It wouldn't have anything to do with a certain handsome rancher, I don't suppose."

Melanie willed her pale cheeks not to reveal her discomfort at Katie's teasing, but she could feel the heat rising despite her best efforts. Katie's giggles followed her into her bedroom. As she changed her gown, she told herself it was just in case they were to run into a client. It would not do to be dressed in a dowdy fashion if they wish to promote their abilities. And no, it did not have anything to do with a certain handsome rancher, she insisted to herself with a wry twist to her lips.

Within moments they were on their way, discussing various upcoming commissions, deciding when Katie would visit the customers to discuss the unknown details.

"Now that we have the new fabric swatches that Mr. Spencer arranged for us, you need to visit Mrs. Spencer once more. It seemed as though she would have commissioned many more frocks if we had a more varied selection. Now that we do, she's sure to place another order."

"You're right. And you've been so speedy on completing the latest orders, even without my help, that we have plenty of room in our schedule." Katie smiled at her kindly. "You do realize how much I appreciate you doing so much for me while my head is in the clouds, don't you?"

"Katie, please, there is no need for your flummery. I cannot even begin to express to you how much your companionship and partnership in this business means to me. I don't know where I would be if not for you. Can you imagine? I don't know what I was thinking when I planned to run this business on my own. I know you had planned to take the teaching position, but it was such a stroke of luck for me that you needed to find other employment."

Katie grimaced. "Well it has certainly worked out for the best for me in the long run as well. While I love children in general and most of the specific children whom I've met from the school, I cannot imagine needing to be with them all day every day. And they are so varying! I'm not sure how the teacher managed to keep all their lessons straight. But he must be doing so since Annie is obviously learning and enjoying her schooling."

"Well there you have it, we are mutually benefited and therefore no thanks are necessary from either of us. We are friends and partners, and we each pick up the other's slack. You might have your head in the clouds, but you are still managing to keep up with the clients quite beautifully. And I'm glad you brought Annie into our home. I didn't think I would be happy about it and had every intention of steering clear of her, but she is a dear, and I'm enjoying having her to myself at times."

Katie's gaze turned teasing once more. "See, that is why you need to snare yourself a suitor. You ought to have some children of your own. They would most definitely grow on you."

Melanie laughed. "Your tune sure has changed since we arrived in Missouri. I was the one telling you that you'd find a mate straight off, and you swore you'd never remarry. Now you think everyone should be paired up."

Katie shrugged and grinned. "I want to share my joy."

"On the other hand, misery does love company," Melanie answered dourly, causing Katie to laugh and stick out her tongue.

They were in high spirits when they arrived at their destination. Once again, by some mysterious manner, their approach had been noticed, and Mr. Miller was striding toward them as they drew near to his front porch. Melanie shaded her eyes and stopped in her tracks.

"I absolutely must know before I perish from curiosity. How do you always know when someone is approaching? Every time I come here, you always seem to be on your way to the house."

Mr. Miller grinned. "I have my ways," he answered vaguely. The rolling of her eyes must have prompted because he elaborated. "Remember, I told you how sensitive the horses' hearing is? When I'm mounted, my horse's reaction tells me something is different. Too, there are often dogs around to alert me to arrivals."

"I had no idea a horse could be used as a watch dog."

"All the more reason to love them." With a pleasant smile, he turned to Katie. "You must be Mrs. Carter. I'm Cole Miller, it's a pleasure to finally meet you."

"It's my pleasure, Mr. Miller. I apologize that it has taken me this long to come by and thank you for helping us out with Annie."

"No thanks necessary, as I've already told Miss Jones. We have agreed that we can help each other out with the children."

Katie's eyes were dancing with mischief as she nodded in agreement. "It's wonderful that you should say so, Mr. Miller. Melanie and I were just discussing that very thing. She told me a little bit about your situation, and we thought it might be a good idea for Mary to come and stay with us for a few days."

Mr. Miller's bright blue eyes focused on Melanie for a moment, and her mouth dried as she tried to interpret his thoughts. It seemed to her as though his gaze had cooled significantly. Consumed with guilt, she lowered her gaze from his. Perhaps he truly had confided in her and had expected to keep it as a confidence. Her face flooded with heat.

Katie must have realized her blunder, and she suavely made a recovery. "Do excuse us if we are speaking out of turn, Mr. Miller. I can assure you that Melanie has not been gossiping around town about your personal affairs, but she did, of course, have to discuss it with me in order to be able to make you such an offer, since we share a home."

"Of course," Mr. Miller replied, his face brightening slightly but still not his usual warm geniality. "Won't you come in and have a cup of tea with my sister? I believe you've met her before, haven't you, Mrs. Carter?"

"Yes, in the schoolyard. Thank you, a cup of tea would be welcomed." Katie's answer was polite, and both women followed him into the house while exchanging confused glances.

Chapter Ten

Cole was quite well aware that his anger was misplaced and disproportionate, but he couldn't seem to simmer it down much. He had poured out his heart to Miss Jones, and it seemed as though she had shared it at her first opportunity. What Mrs. Carter said made complete sense — if she had a solution, she needed to ask her housemate if it was all right with her — but he would have preferred if she had asked him first. He had to ask himself why he was taking it quite so personally. He had assured himself that he didn't have warmer feelings for the woman, but he was starting to think he was lying to himself. Maybe he ought to leave town for a time. He could escort Leandra back to Boston himself and see what sort of women his sister-in-law had picked out for him. If he met them for himself, it might not be such a stretch to consider one as a potential wife.

But then he felt a warm hand on his arm, and he looked down into the brown depths of Miss Jones' concerned gaze. "I'm so sorry if we've offended you. I swear I'm not a gossip. But Katie's a mother. I'm not. I thought she would have some insights."

His heart clenched along with his stomach. He wanted to reassure her that he wasn't angry with her, but he wasn't sure if it was true. He gave her a tight smile instead. No further conversation was possible as Leandra entered the scene.

"Mrs. Carter and Miss Jones. What a pleasure to see you."

Leandra was having a reasonably good day, but she was brittle around the edges, and Cole needed to keep an eye on her. He was glad for Mrs. Carter's outgoing cheerfulness despite her apparent ability to get into other people's business.

"Miss Miller, a pleasure to see you, as well. I must tell you the droll mistake that Miss Jones and I both made. We thought you were your brother's wife when you originally extended the invitation for Annie to come and stay over with Mary."

Leandra's harsh laughter followed. "His wife is dead."

"So we've since found out," Mrs. Carter replied gently.

"But Melanie and I have decided to be friends, so I guess you must be, too. We are Leandra and Melanie."

"How lovely. Then you must call me Katie as all my friends do."

"Very well. I s'pose you ought to call my brother Cole, too."

Cole froze in the act of setting the kettle on the stove. He was grateful for Mrs. Carter's quick, warm chuckle.

"That might be a little too forward for us just yet, Leandra. We've just met him. And since it turns out that he's an eligible bachelor around town, we wouldn't want to set the tongues to wagging."

Cole noticed that Miss Jones had still not uttered a word. He cast a glance from the side of his eye at her. She was pale and taut. He wondered what she was thinking. Leandra quickly filled any silence.

"I've heard the tongues are already wagging about you, Katie. Word is you're courting with the doctor."

"Word does spread quickly in a small town, doesn't it?"

"So, it's true then? I thought he was a confirmed bachelor, wallowing in his grief for his dead wife. He didn't have much more than the time of day for me."

Cole could hear the bitterness in his sister's voice. It was rather a shame and quite unusual that she had remained unmarried out here where single women were so scarce. Perhaps many had made the same mistake that Mrs. Carter had spoken of. And then, once the mistake was cleared up, Leandra's negativity wasn't terribly endearing.

"It does take time to get over one's grief and prepare for a new relationship," Mrs. Carter answered in a soothing tone. "I, myself, had been determined that I would never remarry. But Dr. Jeffries and I found ourselves in the right place at the right time, and the sparks flew. There doesn't seem to be much rhyme or reason to it, does there?"

Cole was glad that his back was still turned towards the women because he couldn't help grinning when he heard his sister's disdainful sniff. She obviously wasn't convinced by Mrs. Carter's cheerful chatter. But she also wasn't overtly rude, despite her precarious sanity.

"I must compliment you on your daughter. We quite enjoyed her when she was here visiting. A very polite little girl." Leandra's tone implied she was surprised by the facts she was stating. Cole again had to choke back his amusement. He didn't want to interrupt or draw attention to himself. He waited to see how their visitors would react.

"Why thank you so much, Leandra, although, as you are no doubt aware, Annie hasn't been with me for very long, so I cannot take credit for what a dear she is. I am so blessed to have her." There was a slight pause before she continued. "I probably shouldn't say that, actually, should I? Since the poor child lost her entire family, I ought not say it's my blessing."

Cole wasn't surprised to hear soft-hearted Miss Jones jump into the conversation finally. "Oh no, Katie, don't say that. You and Annie are a blessing for each other after all the tragedies you both have endured. You are not benefitting from her tragedy just as she is not benefitting from yours. But in your current circumstances, you are making the best of it together."

Cole braced himself as he heard sniffling. Women and their waterworks, he thought with a shudder.

"That was beautifully said, Melanie," Leandra complimented.

Cole finally turned to face the women. Mrs. Carter was clasping Miss Jones' hand while dabbing at her eyes. Miss Jones looked decidedly uncomfortable, and Cole's amusement mounted. He had to clear his throat. This brought three sets of eyes to his. Two sets looked surprised to be reminded of his presence, but Miss Jones looked relieved at the interruption.

"How do you take your tea, Mrs. Carter?" he asked, his tone mundane as though he had no idea what had just transpired. He was pleased to see a spark of amusement brighten Miss Jones' gaze.

"Oh, just strong and black, thank you, Mr. Miller. I think I could use the fortification this afternoon."

"Very well," he turned back to the counter and finished his task. "I'm afraid I don't have anything quite so delicious as the cookies Miss Jones has brought us in the past." He could've bitten off his tongue when he noticed the chagrin filling that lady's face. He quickly continued. "But this raisin bread we baked yesterday isn't too bad."

"Thank you, Mr. Miller, this will be quite lovely." Mrs. Carter seemed to be quite the diplomat. She then began to gently probe his sister. "Melanie told me that you have been caring for Mary since she lost her mama. That was generous of you, Leandra. You must be deeply attached to her."

Leandra shrugged. "She's a very energetic child. She would much rather be with her father than cooped up in the house with me."

"Of course, I think that might come with the age," Mrs. Carter agreed with a smile. "Annie is so full of energy. I don't know how their teacher manages to get any learning into them."

Leandra sniffed again. "I don't really see much getting into Mary."

Cole, used to his sister's cutting remarks, barely registered her words, but both of their visitors looked troubled. It seemed too much for even the gregarious Mrs. Carter, who grew quiet. Cole rather thought it was too much for Miss Jones, which is why it prompted her into speech.

"Mary actually struck me as a very bright girl. I think she will take to her classes very well. I'm just so happy for both Annie and Mary that girls are encouraged to attend the school here in Bucklin and that the teacher seems well inclined to teach his entire class."

"I don't see how much good can come from teaching the boys with the girls. Seems to me that none of them will be able to learn anything that way."

Mrs. Carter had finally recovered her wits. "Since both Annie and Mary are only children, I think it will be good for them to have the experience, don't you?"

"Not really. But it's none of my business anymore, anyway. I suppose my brother has told you I'm finally getting out of here?"

"What do you mean?" Mrs. Carter neither agreed nor denied her knowledge.

"I'm going back to Boston." Finally, his sister seemed happy about something.

The two visitors exchanged a glance that made Cole think they had hoped the subject would come up, but he didn't think they were getting straight to their point when they probed with more questions. "Are you happy to be returning to Boston?" Mrs. Carter's question sounded cautious.

"Delighted," Leandra almost grunted, making it difficult for Cole to maintain a straight face.

"We shall miss you, Leandra," Miss Jones stated in a soft but firm voice. "You must have very mixed feelings on your departure."

"Why would my feelings be mixed? I'm finally getting out of this godforsaken place."

Miss Jones blinked but carried on. "No doubt, you'll miss your brother and Mary. Having been here for a few years, it has surely become home, at least to an extent. Are you not a bit nervous that things have changed in your absence and it won't feel like home anymore?"

"I don't think that's likely."

"I'm glad, then." Her answer was kind and gentle. For all her apparent awkwardness, Miss Jones obviously had a sweet heart. Cole closed his eyes in resistance to the thought.

"Is there anything we can do to help you with your preparations, Leandra? I know you and I have just met, but Melanie and I are both of the mind that women must stick together. We would like to do whatever we can to make it easier for you." Mrs. Carter was brisk and matter of fact.

Leandra's forehead wrinkled as though she didn't understand the question. Mrs. Carter elaborated. "Do you have much to pack? Or would it be beneficial for us to have Mary stay with us for a few days? Would you rather she be here or not when you take your leave?"

Leandra's confusion cleared, and so did Cole's. He deeply appreciated the consideration the women were showing. He agreed with their assessment; it would likely be better if Mary wasn't there when his brother's agents came for Leandra. But it would be best if Leandra didn't realize he was for the idea.

"That's mighty kind of you, Katie. I don't have much to pack, that's for certain. I will need to get all my washing done before I pack, and I would like to leave all the housework done up here for Cole so he won't even notice I'm gone for a while. It might actually be best if the girl isn't underfoot. If it wouldn't be too much trouble for you, of course," she added as an afterthought.

"It would be a pleasure for us to have her. And Annie will love it." Mrs. Carter's answer was immediate and sounded sincere. Again, the two women exchanged brief but significant glances. "How soon do you think you'll be leaving? Should we take Mary home with us now or come back for her in a few days?"

Leandra suddenly must have realized how close her return to Boston really was. For a moment, Cole saw his sister's true self displayed on her face, and his heart lurched. She looked for a moment as though she regretted her departure. But then she blinked and the moment passed. While it had seemed to him that she was at a momentary loss, she now gained in determination.

"Of course, the girl isn't ready to just up and leave. But maybe you could come for her things tomorrow and then collect her after school. That might be the easiest thing. Much like how we took Annie when you were unavailable."

Mrs. Carter blinked in surprise over Leandra's return to vicious manner of speech, but she took it in her stride. "Very well, that seems to be a sound plan. One of us will stop by mid-day to collect Mary's things for an expected stay of a few days." Standing up, Mrs. Carter began to bring their visit to a close; obviously, their purpose in coming had been concluded. "Mr. Miller, if you would like to come and collect her when you're ready, that would be appropriate."

Cole nodded his agreement, unsure how he felt about the managing woman. He was surprised to see Miss Jones' eyes twinkling in amusement once more.

"Thank you for the tea," Miss Jones murmured as she shook his hand briefly before taking her leave.

Cole stood at the window and watched the two women as they walked away. He was envious of the easy camaraderie between them. It was apparent that both women were well grounded intellectually and emotionally. Even Miss Jones, despite her awkwardness. It was in sharp contrast with his sister. He really appreciated what a good listener Miss Jones seemed to be. It would be good for Mary to spend time with the two women as well as Mrs. Carter's daughter. He looked forward to telling Mary when she got home from school.

Chapter Eleven

After glancing at the watch she kept in her small handbag, Melanie suggested they stop to collect Annie on their way past the school. "It's only fifteen minutes until class ends. There's no sense in going home."

Katie agreed but then added, "That was far more fascinating than I expected."

"What was? The fact that I keep my watch in my handbag?"

"Don't play coy, Mel, you know what I mean."

"No, as a matter of fact, I don't. What could you have found fascinating about that poor woman's terrible situation? And poor little Mary, being surrounded by so much negativity! It can't be good for her either."

Katie looked shocked by Melanie's words. "I was certainly not making light of Leandra's illness, nor the impact it's sure to have on Mary. I was just commenting on Mr. Miller's apparent fascination with you. Did you not notice that he could barely keep his eyes off you?"

Melanie felt heat filling her cheeks. "No, I noticed no such thing!" Her declaration seemed to fall on deaf ears as Katie laughed.

"Was that because you were making your own best effort to keep your eyes away from him?"

Now it felt as though her face were on fire, but Melanie tried to brazen it out. "I have no idea what you mean. I maintained my focus on Leandra and our conversation with her."

"Of course, you did, because you are a lovely, loyal friend," Katie replied promptly and sincerely, but then she turned teasing. "But you also have eyes in your head, and they seem to find great appreciation in turning toward the handsome rancher."

Melanie debated with herself for a heartbeat but then she turned to her friend. "Was I so very obvious? I would hate for him to think I was setting my cap at him."

Katie's amusement burst into deep chuckles. "Now you're sounding downright historical! Where did you get that expression from?"

Melanie didn't think her embarrassment could grow any deeper. "I read it somewhere," she replied in a stiff voice.

"Oh, don't take offense, my dear friend, I just couldn't help it. Surely you realize that a good laugh will release all the tension from that dreadful interlude. You are so sweet, you might not have noticed how very dreadful Leandra was toward me."

Melanie couldn't stay offended long and couldn't help but release a few giggles of her own. "How could anyone not take note? She was such a dear the first time I met her, and even today, she didn't seem irked with me, but she certainly seemed to have taken you in dislike. I think it's because of the doctor."

"Well, that much was apparent. I feel badly for her and her situation, but that's no reason to tear down another woman's happiness."

"Oh, please tell me you didn't take her words to heart." Melanie was instantly struck by the unfairness of it all.

"Of course not, I could see through it at once. But it was decidedly uncomfortable. Except for the funny way Mr. Miller kept trying to ignore the conversation completely while still staying around to sneak peeks at you."

"Was he really?" Melanie was torn between denial and wanting to hear more. "I'm dreadful at conversing with him, or anyone for that matter, and of course, I have no wish to marry. But he is so very handsome. It's probably all that hard work and fresh air that must come from being a rancher. And he's so sweet with his daughter. And his kindness toward Annie was heartwarming, too."

Katie laughed again. "Oh my dear friend, I do think you have a bad case."

Melanie laughed as well but still asked, "A bad case of what?"

"The love bug." The way she declared it all drawn out and squeaky made them both fall into a fit of giggles. Melanie was the first to sober.

"I won't be able to see him again. You'll have to be the one to go tomorrow and collect Mary's things. Maybe you can drop in there after you've visited one of our clients."

Katie blinked at her in surprise. "Why ever would you say that? Seems to me you should be all the more anxious to spend more time with the good rancher in his time of need."

Melanie didn't even crack a smile over Katie's words. "It is because of his time of need that he doesn't need me. He needs someone who can socialize and be normal in order to help Mary as she grows. Even someone who would happily bear children with him. That someone isn't me. Mary is a dear girl, and I plan to help her as much as I can, but I'm not normal. I can't help her with social things. And I have absolutely no interest in bringing any babies into this world."

Katie's eyes were kind but damp; she seemed at a loss for words. "Give it time, my dear Mel. You might change your mind. And I think you're completely normal. Just because you would prefer to stay at home doesn't mean there's something wrong with you."

"That's not what my father has said."

"Well your father is a nincompoop, and that's all I plan to say on the subject. Now, come along. We need to fetch Annie from school. And my stomach is starting to growl. Poor Mr. Miller's raisin bread was a touch dry. It was all I could do to get it swallowed, even with his delicious tea."

Melanie didn't bother replying, just picking up her skirts and hurrying beside her friend to fetch their small companion.

Early the next morning, there was a knock on the door. It was Dr. Jeffries stopping in on his way to an emergency, asking Katie to accompany him. As she gathered her things, Katie couldn't quite hide her smile.

"I swear to you, I didn't arrange this. You know I couldn't have, we were together all evening. And I would never implicate the good doctor in any of my schemes, besides. But now you're going to have to go collect Mary's things yourself."

Melanie stood still and blinked, knowing she must appear a simpleton, but there was nothing that could be done, so she tried to figure out the best course of action. "What about the clients you were supposed to visit?"

Katie bit her lip in uncertainty. "I don't have time to send someone with a message. I'm so sorry, Melanie. Do you think you could just stop in to see them and explain that I'll be by tomorrow? Or even later on today if this situation with Dr. Jeffries resolves itself quickly."

Melanie tried to stay calm. She knew Katie would be concerned for her as well as the patient. Biting her lip and trying to be brave, she shooed Katie out the door. "Just remind me the names, and I'll do my best."

"Thank you, Melanie, I'm so sorry to leave you with so many things to take care of. It's Mrs. Jenkins and Mrs. Spencer. I have notes on them on my desk in my room. You're the very best," she called out as she ran out the door after the doctor.

"Yeah, I'm the best idiot in town," Melanie murmured as her stomach churned and a sheen of sweat broke out on her forehead. She tried to decide what to do first. There were no sewing tasks left; she had plowed through all that needed to be done earlier. That was why it was all the more urgent that the clients be visited. They needed more work. The house was spotless, so she couldn't procrastinate under the guise of needing to do chores. With a deep sigh, she realized she needed to tidy herself and get on with the necessary visits.

As she combed her hair, she could see how very pale she was. *You can do this*, she reassured her reflection. After rummaging through Katie's desk, she had all the information she needed. It was time to set off and find someone who could direct her in the way she ought to go.

Standing on her front porch, Melanie took deep fortifying breaths, willing her heart rate to slow down and her feet to hurry up. If she wasn't careful, she would need Dr. Jeffries to pay a call on her before long. Or she'd be dead, she thought with a macabre sense of satisfaction. That would eliminate her responsibility to make these visits, at the very least.

While she was dithering, she almost didn't notice the approaching wagon until it was drawing up on the other side of their little fence.

"Oh Mr. Miller, I'm surprised to see you here." It was a dull-witted thing to say, but it popped out of her mouth without her permission.

"Good-day, Miss Jones. It seems I've just caught you in time. Were you headed our way, by any chance?"

She felt color finally touch her cheeks; hopefully she looked a little less like a corpse. "In a manner of speaking," she replied with amusement filling her tone. "I was trying to decide who to visit first. But I'm pretty sure that you would have had to be my last stop, since I would have things to carry afterward."

"Well, then I'm all the more glad that I've caught you."

His friendly smile and warm voice did a strange combination of settling her nerves and setting them to jangling all at once. Melanie wasn't quite sure how to manage the sensory overload. She merely smiled in return and hoped he would continue talking.

"I didn't want you to have to carry Mary's things, so I've brought them to you."

"Oh, that's so thoughtful of you, thank you so much." Melanie wasn't sure if she should approach him, or wait until he brought the things to her. When he began climbing down from the wagon, she decided to allow her feet to remain planted where they were.

"It's the least I could do since you've been so kind as to get my daughter away from the mess at home. Leandra held her composure fairly well this morning as she said her goodbyes to Mary. Mary seemed confused by the whole thing, though, I'm afraid. You might have some strange questions to handle this afternoon."

Melanie's stomach sank, but she had agreed to the arrangement, so there was nothing to do but assure the man. "I'm sure we'll manage to muddle through."

"Are you sure you're up to it, Miss Jones? You're looking a little more pale than usual. Are you feeling poorly?"

Melanie could feel color flooding her cheeks, putting the lie to his observation. But the sudden change made her feel suddenly lightheaded. She must have wobbled where she stood because Mr. Miller put his hand out to grasp her arm.

"Perhaps you should be sitting in the shade. The heat must be getting to you." He guided her gently toward one of the chairs she and Katie had placed in the shade of the covered porch.

Despite allowing him to direct her to a seat, Melanie protested. "No, no, I'm fine. It isn't even really all that hot."

"Well then what's wrong? Can I assist you in some way?"

His kindness made her want to weep. She hoped her chin didn't tremble.

"You are being exceedingly kind, Mr. Miller, I thank you. But I don't think there's anything you can do. I need to face my demons on my own." She avoided his gaze by putting the small sack he handed her inside the front door before closing it again behind her.

His compassionate gaze made her wish she could unburden herself, but she resisted. She had made that mistake in the past. She had no interest in repeating it.

"That sounds mighty serious. What sort of demons might a sweet woman like yourself be running from?"

Finally, she couldn't fight the temptation to share her burdens any longer, and tears welled up over her lids. She wanted to drop through the floor of the porch for turning into a weeping ninny in front of the sturdy man, but the expression on his face looked so much like understanding that she just couldn't resist.

"I have to go visit our clients," she finally answered him. She could hear the despair in her voice and would have found it amusing if it weren't truly how she felt. She felt despair over having to go speak to strangers. But it was obvious the steadfast man before her didn't understand what she was saying. He stared at her in anticipation of further explanation.

"I'm terrified, and I was trying to talk myself into stepping off the porch when you arrived."

His smile curdled the edges of her stomach. "And I went ahead and interrupted you. I sincerely do apologize, Miss Jones. I hope I haven't set you back too much."

Melanie couldn't help returning his smile. "Well, I hadn't made much progress. I had been standing on the porch for at least ten minutes when you arrived."

"Is there a particular reason why you are so mighty frightened of visiting your clients? Have they been particularly unpleasant? I wouldn't expect you need to keep a client that abuses you." His eyes were kind as he tried to understand her predicament.

Melanie hesitated but finally blurted the truth. "I haven't even met them, so no, they haven't been abusive. In fact, Katie, I mean Mrs.

Carter, has already met both of the women I am supposed to be visiting and enjoyed them very much. In fact, she considers Mrs. Jenkins to be a personal friend by now."

"Well, I've met Mrs. Jenkins, and I could understand why a body might be a little nervous of encountering her. She has a certain personality that might not sit right with just anyone."

Melanie began to relax, just as he had obviously intended. She even mustered up a chuckle over his description of Mrs. Jenkins. "Yes, Katie told me of her first encounters with Mrs. Jenkins. But she truly sounds like a dear old soul. I just really don't like meeting new people."

Mr. Miller's forehead crinkled in concern. "Do you truly have to go, then? If Mrs. Carter usually makes these visits, why don't you leave it until she can follow up? You don't need to work yourself up into a taking over it."

⚜

Cole watched as the pretty woman stared out into the vista. He was fairly certain she was pondering his words. His heart wrenched for her. He couldn't quite relate to her fears, but it was obvious she was nervous of people. He couldn't help but notice it the very first day they had met. But she always seemed to handle herself well despite those nerves. Clearly, he didn't fully understand her situation.

She finally broke her silence. With a low voice she said, "I'm afraid if I don't do it now, I'll be stuck in this house forever, and then of what use will I be to anyone, including myself?"

He shocked himself by realizing that he was filled with pride for her brave effort, even though he still didn't understand.

"Besides, I'll be letting down Katie and Annie. We need the work to be able to support ourselves. I don't really care for myself, but we need to keep our clients happy in order to keep business coming. Something came up for Katie this morning, an emergency that the doctor needed her help with. She had promised these two women she would visit them. I need to at least let them know that she'll stop by another day. We've already done work for each of them, you see. I can't let any of them down."

Cole admired her diligence, but he wondered if perhaps it was part of her problem. "Seems to me like you might be putting too much pressure on the situation. Is it really so very vital that these clients get visited today? What would happen if you don't?"

He watched as she chewed her lip, deep in thought. The desire to run his thumb across the abused lip, to sooth it and her, overwhelmed him. He resisted the urge, unsure if he liked the fluttering in his midsection as he watched her but knew his feelings were becoming engaged whether he wanted them to or not.

"Since there wasn't a seamstress in town before we arrived, no, you're probably right, nothing dire would happen. It's not as though they can take their business elsewhere. But it's important to both Katie and me to keep our word. And we also believe that if we are reliable, it'll make the ladies more inclined to place orders, you know? I mean, if it's a truly positive experience for them, they'll want to repeat it."

Cole nodded, understanding her insistence on making her visits. "If it means that much to you, then why are you so nervous about it? Doesn't your motivation overpower your hesitance?"

"I was hoping it would," she answered, her glum tone making him want to smile, but he resisted, sparing her feelings. He was rewarded by her further words as she gazed out into the yonder once more. "I don't really even remember how it started. Probably some snide remark as I walked Henry to school. But I became more and more nervous about going outside. I forced myself for Henry's sake, but I was never so relieved as when he finally insisted that he was too big to be walked to school anymore. I didn't completely agree that he was big enough, but our father sided with him, and then I didn't have to make myself do it anymore."

"Was your father just trying to spare your feelings?"

The laughter that answered his question was bitter. "Certainly not. If he knew how much I dreaded the morning visits, he would have insisted Henry still needed to be escorted to this day, even though the boy is sixteen."

Cole blinked, wondering how anyone could mistreat this sweet woman. "But you're such a strong, determined female. I'm surprised the murmurings of a few nasty women would tie you up into such a knot."

Her smile was gentle as she finally met his gaze. "That's kind of you to say, Mr. Miller, but I don't really think I'm that strong. And the mothers at school were only the start of my problem. It grew exponentially when I was beaten and robbed while going for the shopping one day just after I had dropped Henry at school. I was fifteen. I should've known how rough the neighborhood was that I was walking through. And I shouldn't have walked through it. But I was rushing to get things done because I had promised one of the upstairs neighbors to help her with something, and my father expected all my chores to be finished before I thought of doing anything else."

Cole was shocked speechless when she said she had been beaten and robbed. It was all he could do not to pull her into his arms and try to soothe away the memories. "Were you very badly injured?"

Her answering shrug didn't really tell him much. "It could've been much worse, I've been assured. At least they didn't assault me in other ways, besides taking my money and punching and kicking me." She was quiet for a moment before adding, "But my father's anger was almost as bad."

"Did he hit you, too?" Cole became enraged.

"No. But sometimes I wished he would and get it over with. I've learned from experience that words can hurt as much as physical blows." Her soft, sweet voice belied the harsh words.

Cole had never felt so inclined to violence in his life. If her father were before him in that moment, he wasn't sure if he would be able to resist giving the man a taste of his own actions.

Reaching out, Cole took one of her hands gently into his large one. Looking at it, it wasn't much bigger than Mary's, but the feelings inspired in him were most certainly not paternal. "I can certainly understand now why you were nervous about going outside in New York after the experiences you've had, but surely you know those bullies aren't here."

She met his eyes, and hers were full of pain. "The mind doesn't always make the most sense, though, does it? Just look at your sister."

"Your situation doesn't seem anything like Leandra's."

"Maybe not, but it's still all in both of our heads. I know those boys who beat me are not here in Bucklin. And my father is dead. But leaving our apartment had become such an ordeal that the feelings have spilled over to here."

"I'm rather amazed that you actually got up the gumption to get on the train and come to Missouri."

She grinned. "So am I." She laughed a little before adding, "But staying was worse, so I was able to just do it. Some days I don't know how I managed. But I'm grateful that I did." She paused again, avoiding his gaze. "Now all I have to do is make sure I don't turn into a house-bound crazy woman out here in Missouri."

"Well, I for one, am convinced you are not crazy. You have been dealt some dreadful circumstances and have managed quite well, from what I can see."

Her surprise was written all over her face as she turned her puzzlement toward him. "How can you say that? I've just explained to you how terrified I am to visit two women, who are reportedly either quite nice or at least quite unlikely to do me any harm."

"You might be terrified, but here you are dressed and ready to go make those very same visits."

His admiration must have finally gotten through to her. She grinned. "True. But I am still here on my own porch."

"That's only because you were interrupted. Now, I probably shouldn't take any more of your time. Would you like me to drop you off at your first destination?"

She was again back to chewing on her lip. Cole was surprised to realize he was still holding her hand. He wasn't sure why it surprised him. He still hadn't grown used to the warm press of it against his own. And the flutters in his stomach hadn't abated, perhaps they had grown worse. She didn't seem at all affected by his presence as he was by hers. That was disheartening.

"Won't that cause gossip? I think the townspeople are already buzzing about Katie. I wouldn't want them thinking New York women were loose."

Cole grinned and squeezed her hand. "I don't think you know very much about loose women if you think accepting a ride on my very open wagon would make you so."

He was gratified to see that her color had returned to normal from the dreadful paleness she had been displaying when he had arrived. Now her cheeks flushed a becoming pink in understanding of his meaning.

"Well, no, of course not," she stammered. "But I don't want you put into an uncomfortable position. My father hated when tales were brought back to him."

"I can assure you, I am nothing like your father. And you will recall that I'm the one who extended the invitation."

Now she looked truly embarrassed, which had definitely not been his intention. But she looked so adorable as her eyes bounced around, looking for anywhere else to gaze rather than at him. "It's kind of you to offer, thank you, Mr. Miller. It might give me just that last little bit of gumption I was looking for."

Cole laughed. "Or at the very least, get you started on the way rather than with your feet glued to your porch."

Her eyes once again came to rest on his face. He was surprised to see another smile on her face. "Whatever works, right?" she asked. "I am determined to grow a spine while living here in Bucklin."

"I think your spine is already made of steel, Miss Jones. You are truly brave to come out here to a new life and face your fears."

"Do you really think so?" she asked, her voice sounding breathless, as though she couldn't quite believe her ears.

"I truly do."

"But I've been wondering if coming out here is just another way of hiding from my fears."

Now he was puzzled. "What are you hiding from here? It seems to me you faced your fear of strangers by getting on a train and moving to a new place."

She was frowning in concentration as she nodded in response to his words. "I also couldn't bear to see my baby brother, whom I raised by my own hand from when I was ten years old, turning into an exact replica of our father."

Cole turned so that he was fully facing her, grasping both of her hands in his own. She couldn't avoid his gaze any longer but was instead searching his face with concern etched upon her own.

"Miss Jones, or rather, I am going to be so bold as to use your given name, Melanie, listen to me carefully. Having the dignity to leave a bad situation is not giving in to fear. It is true bravery when considered along with your fears. I am in awe of you right at this moment."

She continued to search his face as though to determine the sincerity of his words. Cole wasn't sure what she read in his features but suddenly, tears spilled over her lashes and trickled down her cheeks. "That is the loveliest thing anyone has said to me in my entire life. Thank you, Mr. Miller."

"Please, you must call me Cole."

Now she was back to blushing as she tried to pull her hands out of his grasp. "Oh no, I wouldn't think that's appropriate."

He ignored her words, merely transferring one of her hands into the grasp of the other, using his free hand to wipe the tears from her cheeks. "I most certainly think it's appropriate, at least when it's just the two of us. We are friends after all, aren't we?"

Cole decided to take a step back for a moment from the lovely woman. While he knew his heart was becoming quite entwined with her, he was well aware that she wasn't anywhere near ready for a declaration from him. She probably wasn't even aware of his feelings or of the fact that he had been holding her hand for the last ten minutes, at least. With a gentle smile, he squeezed her hands and then let them go.

"Come along, Miss Mel, I'll drop you off with either Mrs. Jenkins or Mrs. Spencer. Which would you like to visit first?"

His tone brooked no argument and did the trick. She got to her feet and accepted that he was going to help her. She still appeared undecided as to her destination, but then she surprised him by answering firmly. "Since Mrs. Jenkins might be the toughest visit, I'll start there, I think. Thank you, again, Cole. It seems all I'm doing of late is thanking you for something."

He grinned over her use of his name but waved off her thanks. "You are doing me a massive favor in keeping Mary for a few days. Dropping you off somewhere on my way home is the very least I can do. It would be churlish not to, really."

Her giggle met his words, for which he was grateful.

They chatted about inconsequential things as they drove out to Mrs. Jenkins' neat property. She and her husband had a good amount of land, but it was currently being worked by her son-in-law. What she had kept for herself was well maintained, despite her age and declining health.

In his effort not to overwhelm Melanie with his attentions, he didn't get out of the wagon, just leaned down to hold her steady as she climbed down on her own.

Her eyes twinkled at him, despite the fact that he could see the nerves returning to her face. "Since you said no thanks are allowed, I will merely wish you a good day. Please, call around when you're ready to have Mary returned to you. Don't feel obliged to rush. We will enjoy having her for however long you deem fit."

Cole was surprised by her offer, especially when he knew she had been hesitant in agreeing to his original request for her help with Mary. He squeezed her hand and then let it go.

"Take care," was all he said as he stirred up his horses to carry on.

The tiny little woman who opened the door at Melanie's knock was a surprise. From all Katie's talk of Mrs. Jenkins' personality, Melanie had expected a larger woman.

"Good day, ma'am, are you Mrs. Jenkins?"

"That I am, and who might you be?"

"I'm Melanie Jones. You are more acquainted with my business partner, Mrs. Katie Carter."

"I know who you are. It's about time you stopped in to visit me. I was starting to think you were a figment of Katie's imagination, just a convenient excuse when she needs to make a decision. She's forever saying, 'oh I have to check with my partner on that.' I wasn't convinced there was any such partner."

The older woman's cackling laugh made Melanie's nerves tighten further, but she obediently followed when Mrs. Jenkins waved her into the sitting room. "You'll bide a while for a cup of tea, won't you? I suppose you're here to tell me Katie won't be stopping by, am I right?"

She barely allowed Melanie an opportunity to nod before she was off and talking again. "Katie always sits and has a visit with me whenever she stops by, so I baked up some biscuits, since she told me she'd be by today and that she enjoys my biscuits. Since she couldn't be bothered to come herself, we shan't have to save her any."

Another cackle accompanied these words, but Melanie was finally able to relax a little bit when she realized that the woman's bark was most definitely worse than her bite.

"Katie felt dreadful that she wasn't able to keep her appointment with you, but she was called out on an emergency with the doctor."

Mrs. Jenkins sniffed. "Far be it from me to begrudge the good doctor from someone in need, but I hardly see how he was in such dire need of Katie's assistance. He managed just fine on his own before she arrived in town. Seems to me that it's just a convenient excuse for the two of them to spend time together making calf's eyes at each other."

Melanie couldn't help a snort of laughter that escaped, making her feel highly disloyal toward her friend. She didn't want to agree with the other woman, but really, she was right. Dr. Jeffries seemed to have managed just fine before they arrived. But they did appear to be deeply in love, and Melanie couldn't begrudge it to them. Thankfully, aside from a delightful grin in response to Melanie's snort, Mrs. Jenkins didn't seem to require any response and just carried on talking.

"It's just as well that Katie wasn't able to come and you felt an obligation to take her place. I've been wanting to meet you, if you did turn out to be a real person. And here you are. And was that Cole Miller dropping you off? You girls certainly haven't been wasting any time in the gentleman department, have you? You just pull up in the train, and you capture all our best bachelors."

By now Melanie felt as though her face were on fire. She tried to stammer out a reply. "Oh, no, Mrs. Jenkins, it just so happened that Mr. Miller was heading this way, and he offered to give me a ride. There is nothing more to it than that."

"Where was he going that he was heading in this direction?" Mrs. Jenkins sounded suspicious.

"I believe he was going home." Melanie could hear how weak her explanation sounded and tried not to cringe.

"Well I'm most certainly not on his way home," Mrs. Jenkins responded, a note of glee in her voice. "Sounds to me like you and Mr. Miller are smelling of April showers."

Melanie blinked. She'd never heard the expression before but from the context, it was rather apparent what the older woman was implying. But Melanie refused to accept such an implication. She decided to brazen it out. "Whatever do you mean by saying this? It's nearly June, isn't it Mrs. Jenkins?"

Another cackle came in response. "I like you, Miss Jones. You've got a backbone for all your apparent timidity. Now, tell me about yourself."

Thus admonished, and relieved that the old woman was willing to leave off teasing her about Cole, Melanie launched into an abbreviated explanation of her life and how she wound up here in Bucklin, Missouri. As she was telling the older woman a much less detailed version than she had shared with Cole, Melanie couldn't believe that she had revealed so much to the handsome man. What must he think of her? She asked herself at the back of her mind, hoping her inner turmoil wasn't revealing itself to Mrs. Jenkins. Some of it must have because Mrs. Jenkins was much more sympathetic than Melanie would have expected.

"You've definitely had your share of loss in your life, haven't you, dear?"

Melanie blinked, trying not to show how deep was her surprise. "Well, many have had more loss than I have, just look at Katie and Annie."

"It speaks well of you that you would say that, dearie, but it doesn't change the fact that you've experienced heartache. More than many, I dare say. It's no wonder you don't want to go out amongst folks. You're still in mourning, aren't you?"

Melanie blinked again. "I hadn't thought of it quite that way, but I dare say you're right. Thank you, Mrs. Jenkins. That was actually quite a helpful observation."

Mrs. Jenkins cackled again. "Well, I don't see as how, but I'm glad you thought so. Now, tell me whatever message my friend Kate had for me. Are you here to show me more samples and badger me into ordering more gowns?"

"We would never badger a client, Mrs. Jenkins," Melanie replied with dignity before laughing a little. "But I do have some samples with me that Katie thought might interest you."

"She knows I can't resist now that I've gotten used to these nice things you've made. Make yourself useful and make us some tea while I'll look them over."

Melanie, feeling lighter than she had in ages, bustled about the tidy kitchen, admiring its size and the convenient location of things. It was obviously a well-used room in the house that had raised a large family.

Her visit with Mrs. Jenkins came to a conclusion well before Melanie felt the need to watch the clock. As she walked away, hopefully in the right direction, Melanie couldn't believe how comfortable she had been with the seemingly cranky old woman. She hoped her next visit went as smooth.

She had to ask for directions on the way to the Spencer house, but the couple had been kind and direct, and Melanie arrived on Mrs. Spencer's front porch without too much difficulty. Taking a deep breath, she knocked firmly, not allowing herself time to second guess the decision.

A tall woman with unruly curls and a wide smile opened the door almost immediately. Her face fell slightly when she saw Melanie. "Oh, I was expecting someone else. Hello."

Melanie couldn't help a chuckle. "Good day, Mrs. Spencer, I'm sorry for the disappointment. I'm Melanie Jones, Mrs. Carter's business partner. Katie has been called away to an important assignment, so I have stopped by in her stead. If you would prefer to speak with her, that is perfectly all right. But neither of us wanted you to be waiting for her and her not turn up."

"No, no, that's quite all right," the woman answered as she opened the door wide, waving Melanie to come in. "I'm just as glad to get to meet you. There are never enough women in town, so the chance to meet a new one is a treat I won't pass up, to be sure. Do come in and have a cup of tea."

Melanie grinned. She hadn't realized how much tea Katie must have to drink in the course of her day when she was visiting the clients. No wonder she sometimes declined the offer when it was just the two of them at home. She didn't tell any of that to Mrs. Spencer, of course. "Thank you, that's kind of you to offer," was the only possible answer.

With Mrs. Spencer being a bit of a chatterbox, Melanie didn't have to make any effort as she listened to the gregarious blonde woman tell her all about her life and how she came to be in Bucklin.

"And what a wonderful surprise to find the two newest women to town are fine seamstresses! You would never believe just how happy that has made me," the pretty blonde declared.

"Well, I am glad to be able to fill a need."

"Oh dear me, a need is an understatement. I can barely sew on a button, so I was of no use to myself. All my pretty things that I have had since moving here were beginning to wear, and what was I to do? I didn't feel I could go to the tailor, although I know a few of the other ladies in town have done so, merely out of desperation, of course. But you two arrived before I had to sink to that level, praise be."

The woman rubbed her hands together, much like a child in anticipation of a treat. "Now tell me, do you have some new samples for me? Katie assured me more cloth would be arriving from Boston on the train, but I was trying not to get my hopes up too high. I'm sure anything silk would be just too much to ask for out here in the back of beyond."

Melanie's heart sank. Katie hadn't told her the woman was expecting silks. She would have to use whatever skills of diplomacy she could muster. Pasting a smile onto her face, Melanie was quick to pull out her swatches.

"No silks yet, I'm afraid, but I'm sure this blue would look wonderful on you. Let me show you what we have."

With a squeal, the woman happily plunked down on the settee beside Melanie and grabbed the bundle from her hands.

"You are quite right, this is the exact color I was looking for. It will be my new special occasions dress. Thank you. Katie has told me that the fancier stitches are your work. What do you think you can do with this for me?"

With that, they launched into a surprisingly enjoyable discussion of the merits of various stitches and tucks and what the woman expected. For someone who claimed to have no skill, she was certainly very knowledgeable about sewing. Melanie was shocked to see that an hour had already passed by the time they had ironed out all the details of what Mrs. Spencer was looking for in her new gown.

Coming to her feet, Melanie said, "I don't wish to occupy too much of your day, Mrs. Spencer. I apologize if I have overstayed."

"Not at all, Miss Jones, I assure you. It has been my pleasure to make your acquaintance. I don't wish to see an end to Mrs. Carter's visits, but I do hope you'll stop in from time to time as well, even if we don't have swatches to coo over."

Melanie chuckled over the woman's word choice. She didn't make any promises, but she thought she might be able to manage becoming friends with the outgoing woman. It certainly wouldn't require too much effort on her part, Melanie thought with satisfaction, as long as she could get off her own front porch.

Her feet felt lighter and her steps jauntier as she made her way briskly home. She had enjoyed a glorious day. Melanie realized she owed a great deal of it to Cole. She really ought to be still referring to him as Mr. Miller, even in her own mind. It wouldn't do to become overly familiar. But, oh, it had felt so comforting to have his large, warm hand clasping hers that morning as she poured out her woes. And he had been remarkably understanding.

No man she had ever come across had ever been so accepting of a woman's thoughts and feelings. Not even dear Mr. Brace at the orphanage she had volunteered at in New York City. While he was the dearest, kindest man she had ever met, Melanie had never felt inclined to tell Mr. Brace all her concerns. She had always felt he was already carrying the weight of too many with all the poor children to care for, she had felt no inclination to add her own burdens to his broad shoulders.

But with Cole that morning, it had been so different. Even though she was well aware that he had cares of his own with his poor motherless daughter and his sister with the precarious mental health, he had seemed so very receptive to her cares and concerns, not making her feel belittled even when he didn't understand what she was trying to say. It had been glorious really. Even better than talking with Katie, which Melanie found surprising and would have thought impossible if she hadn't experienced it for herself. But his perspective was welcome and she had appreciated his matter of fact help. She just hoped she hadn't made him sick of her when he thought on it later. Melanie refused to dwell on that possibility. She hurried home, determined to get a start on the various commissions from her two visits before she went to collect the little girls from school.

Chapter Twelve

The days flew by in a blur. The four females fell into a comfortable morning routine as they grew accustomed to Mary's presence in the small house. She was a cooperative little girl and seemed thrilled with her adjusted temporary circumstances. It didn't even seem to bother her that her father hadn't returned to collect her. There had only been one awkward conversation wherein she had expressed concerns for her aunt.

"She never really liked me much, but I feel bad that she's sick," Mary had said to Melanie on the first day as they walked home from school.

"Oh, my dear, I think her sickness is why she might have seemed not to like you at times. I'm certain your aunt loved you very much. That's why she stayed here with you and your father even though she was pining for Boston."

Mary's forehead and nose crinkled. "Why would she want to live in a stinky old city? Isn't it so much better here?"

Melanie laughed. "I agree with you, wholeheartedly, Mary, but not everyone sees it quite the same way as we do. There are certain conveniences that people enjoy in the city that we can't get here in Missouri."

"Like what?"

Melanie thought of Mrs. Spencer's silks but didn't think that would be the right explanation. "Well, in the city you can buy anything you might imagine. Here in Missouri, you will most likely have to make it for yourself or go without."

The little girl pondered that for a moment but didn't seem satisfied with it. "I think we have absolutely everything we could possibly need right here in Bucklin."

"Well, I must admit that I agree with you completely, Mary, but there are some people that might find it more work living here than in the city. I remember in New York, you could buy just about anything. You didn't have to have a cow if you wanted milk, and you didn't have to even have an oven if you wanted bread. All you needed was money."

"But how could you get money if you didn't have milk to sell?" The little girl's puzzled frown made Melanie want to smile, but she managed to contain her amusement.

"Back East there are large buildings were many people work all day making things. They get paid by the owner of the building."

Mary still didn't look convinced. "That sounds terr'ble."

Now Melanie did laugh. "I have to say that I feel the same way. But it works for some people. Some don't want to work with animals and are afraid of being outside the city, I think. I'm not really sure what your aunt's thoughts were on the subject, but she truly is pining for the city. That's why she has gotten so sick. So maybe she'll get better now that she's going back."

"Won't she miss us, though?" Mary asked in a small voice.

"Once she gets settled, I'm sure she will. She might even regret her choice to return. But for now, she truly believes it will make her happy, and we need to be glad for her that she's getting her wish. And we also should be grateful that she stayed as long as she did."

"How come?"

"Can you imagine what your papa would have done with a tiny baby by himself and with all the chores to do? Would you have wanted to be in the barn with him in your baby pajamas?"

The droll tone she used as she asked the questions helped the little girl find her humor, and she giggled along with Annie, who had joined the conversation.

"Well, I do love being in the barn with my papa now, but maybe it's not the right place for a baby."

"See, exactly, that's why we need to be thankful that Aunt Leandra came and looked after you and the house when your father needed the help. Now you're a big girl and in school for a good part of the day, so she can return to her own affairs."

They walked along in silence for a few minutes. Melanie noticed that the little girl still looked troubled.

"Are you thinking that you're going to miss your aunt?"

"I'm not sure," the child admitted. "Sometimes I wish she would go away, but now that it's here I feel sad."

"That's natural. Now that you're in school, you'll learn to write so you can stay in touch with her through letters. Maybe when your aunt is well and you're a little older, the two of you will be able to visit each other in person."

This seemed to lighten the girl's burdened heart, and she was able to play and giggle along with Annie as they skipped the rest of the way home.

Melanie, watching them play, couldn't help but be relieved that she had crossed the emotional hurdle with the youngster. She knew the child's father was relying on her to help in such a way, and she had worried she would be inadequate to the task. Thankfully, Mary was a sweet, biddable child with a kind heart. She wouldn't be a burden to spend time with.

A week had passed by the time Cole called round to collect his daughter. Melanie had half expected him on the weekend so was surprised when he didn't turn up until Tuesday to collect Mary's things while the girls were in school.

Melanie was glad that Katie was home, so it wasn't inappropriate to invite him in for a cup of tea while Mary's things were gathered.

"We were getting quite used to having her with us. It will take some adjusting to having her gone," Melanie remarked as she set the kettle to boil and then quickly folded Mary's spare clothes and placed them in a bag.

"And Annie will be disappointed not to have her playmate at home with her," Katie added from her place by the window where she was hemming a client's gown.

"Thank you for your kindness, Mrs. Carter and Miss Jones. I never meant to prevail upon your hospitality for quite this long."

"Did things proceed in a more complicated manner than you had expected?" Melanie asked softly.

"Leandra didn't take too well to being collected by strangers. She felt it made her seem like a disobedient child, she said. She refused to go at first. She missed the train they had planned to take. Leandra wore herself out with her protests but then in a lucid moment, she realized it was ridiculous to object to the manner of departure. She really had no desire to remain here, so why was she putting up such a fuss? She got on the train this morning, and I pretty much came straight here."

"I'm so sorry that it was such an ordeal for both of you." Melanie's heart ached.

"Well, I'm beyond grateful that you two had the sense to realize it might be difficult and keeping Mary well away from it."

"She was a pleasure to have. We'll be sad to see her go."

"I appreciate you saying that, but I'll be glad to have her back."

Melanie laughed. "We weren't thinking to steal her from you, have no fear."

They shared a chuckle and a cup of tea before the rancher set off for his own place after assuring them he'd be early to the school after classes so Mary would realize she was to go home with him.

Melanie was watching him drive away through the front window that overlooked the porch when she heard a girlish giggle from behind her. She whirled around, knowing a frown was pulling on her forehead.

"What's so funny?" Melanie was confused.

"You are, silly." Katie's answer was impossible to misunderstand.

"Why would you say that?"

"For all your protestations that you have no interest in the handsome Mr. Miller, you sure couldn't tear your eyes away from his back as he drove away."

Melanie knew her face was bright red with her embarrassment. What was there to say? She had stood there fawning over the man like a teenager rather than the sensible woman she thought she was. Katie must've realized she had no answer, and she broke the silence.

"There is nothing to be ashamed of, Mel, surely you realize that. You are a single woman with no obligations to hold you back from pursuing a relationship. Mr. Miller is a fine man from what I can tell. He, too, is single and only has responsibility for a sweet child that you seem to already care about. What seems to be the trouble?"

Melanie huffed and sat limply at the table. She felt helpless and didn't know how to answer her friend.

"I gave all I had to give to my little sister and brother. I did my very best for them and my father. But I ended up lonely and shunned for my efforts. My father couldn't even be bothered to name me in his will, leaving everything he possessed to Henry. And Henry has no use for me now that he feels he's a grown man at the ripe age of sixteen." Melanie paused as she wiped a tear from her cheek. "I don't know if I have anything left in my heart to give anyone, Kate."

Soft-hearted Katie gripped Melanie's hand tight and allowed her own tears to flow in sympathy. "You are a dear, and I know you have a heart full of love to share. Just look how you've taken to Annie even though you said you didn't want any responsibility."

"Well, I don't have any responsibility, she's your daughter."

"But with how side-tracked I am by the doctor, you're the one carrying the load most of the time." Katie's grin showed she had no resentment for her friend's care of her daughter.

Melanie shrugged. "It's different to help when it's not my own responsibility. I don't know if I can take on being a mother for real."

Katie nodded, clearly in thought. "There's one thing I think you should give thought to, before you dismiss the idea entirely. You were too young for the responsibilities you had to take on when your mother died. You did the very best you could, and it seems to me if your sister is married and your brother on his own, you must have done a fine job with them, even if you aren't too happy with your brother's personality. You did the best you could while dealing with the bad influence of a mean-spirited father. As a grown woman, if you have a loving partner to share the responsibility, I do think you would find the experience to be far different and much more rewarding than raising your brother and sister in a cramped apartment in the city."

Melanie didn't feel convinced, but she knew there was wisdom in her friend's words. "I think I'll go for a walk. I will mull over your words."

Katie nodded and returned to her hemming. "Don't feel you need to hurry back. I'll be able to collect Annie today. I'm sure she'll be disappointed that Mary won't be coming home with us, so I'll need to spend some time with her."

Melanie absently nodded her agreement and slipped through the front door, already lost in thought.

Chapter Thirteen

A few weeks slowly slipped past. Melanie made every effort to convince herself that she was satisfied with the routine that had settled over her life. Her first venture toward visiting clients had not been her last, even though Katie looked after most of that side of the business. Melanie was happy that she was slowly regaining confidence in her ability to speak with people, even strangers. She still got nervous, but it was not debilitating.

Katie was so often wandering away for walks with Doctor Jeffries that Melanie spent a great deal of time with Annie. Melanie had to make herself keep a rein on her love for the little girl. With the way Katie's relationship was progressing with the doctor, Melanie was sure it wouldn't be too very much longer before Katie and Annie were no longer her housemates. Melanie's heart ached at the thought of being alone. She had always thought it would be her greatest joy to be on her own, but she now saw that it would be sad and lonely.

Perhaps I ought to send to Mr. Brace for an orphan of my own, she thought one day as she watched Annie and Mary carefully cutting out cookies as she had instructed them. Mary had come home with Annie to spend the weekend with them once more. It had become another routine for them. Mary came every second weekend, coming home from school with Annie and staying until they went back to school on Monday. *As she supervised, her thoughts wandered to the last time she had seen Mary's father, a few days prior.*

Melanie was so surprised by the knock on her door that she almost put the needle through her finger. Shaking her head at herself, she hurried toward the door. She was surprised again to see that it was Mr. Miller on the porch when she opened the door.

"Hello," she said, cringing when she heard how breathy she sounded.

"Good day," he answered, touching the brim of his hat politely before lifting his other hand and showing her the sacks he held. "I've come to help you move the flowers you were talking about."

Melanie blinked at him. "I can't believe you remembered my saying that."

To her surprise, the man actually blushed.

"You've been doing so much for my Mary, I was trying to think of something I could do for you, and then I remembered that conversation we had." He ducked his head, clearly embarrassed. "If you'll just point me in the right direction of which ones you wanted moved, I could have it done in a flash."

Melanie was skeptical. "I don't see how it could be a quick task, Mr. Miller. The plants I like have thorns on them. Surely that will complicate matters considerably."

He just shrugged. "I have gloves."

Now she was getting excited and allowed a grin to spread over her face. "If you're very sure, I would love to have two of those prickly bushes with the bright red flowers brought here on either side of the stairs."

"Only two? That will be easy as pie."

"Maybe meringue pie," Melanie replied with a laugh. "Making meringue is hard."

"You needn't do anything but point me in the direction of the plants you want. I promise, I don't think it'll be difficult."

Melanie offered no further protests, delighted at the thought of having the bright splash of color in front of her small house. Her heart beat raced far out of proportion to the slow pace they set as they walked toward the wild flower patch behind her house. She was grateful he adjusted his long stride so she didn't have to run to keep up with him.

She tried not to stare at his handsome physique. His generous act of kindness toward her was not helping her keep her feelings in check toward him, Melanie realized and tried to distract her thoughts with light chatter as she watched him work. The play of his muscles easily viewed, even under his shirt as he dexterously dug, made her heart flutter and her palms sweat. Melanie again tried to keep herself from looking.

True to his word, before too long both small bushes were nicely positioned at the bottom of the stairs. She didn't think she had laughed so much before in her life. She was feeling absolutely giddy in the handsome man's presence. Melanie tried to keep a rein on her bubbling emotions, but her lessened anxieties in connection with people seemed to be spilling over into increased attraction. She would absolutely die of mortification if he thought she was throwing herself at him, so she tried to keep the volume of her giggles as low as possible.

As she was shaking his hand in thanks once more while he was taking his leave, she noticed he had sustained a couple scratches despite his thick gloves.

"Oh, no, Mr. Miller, I just knew it was going to be a detrimental exercise."

"Don't you pay those marks any mind. I've had far worse from the barn cats, I can assure you. I'm just glad you're pleased with my little contribution."

Melanie clasped her hands in front of her and beamed at him. "I am most definitely pleased. I thank you from the bottom of my heart."

Again, she was surprised to see a blush staining his cheeks. He looked bashful but didn't say anything more, only touching the brim of his hat again and waving as he drove off.

The girls' giggles brought her back to the present with a slight sigh.

Melanie enjoyed the chatter of the two little girls as she taught them how to cook and bake. She was also trying to teach them how to sew, but Mary especially found the task tedious at best. She would far rather be out working with her father on his ranch, but it would seem Mr. Miller was determined that his daughter get at least some education in the female arts, as he liked to put it. Melanie had to guard her heart from growing too attached to both girls. *I'll write to Mr. Brace and the Children's Aid Society first thing tomorrow,* Melanie thought as she watched them try not to spill too much flour around the tidy kitchen.

₧₧

"I can't believe she was once the one insisting that we needed to play tea parties. Now she wishes she was a boy." The rancher shook his head in confusion as he sat with Melanie when he had finally come round to call several weeks later. No one else was home so Melanie hadn't invited him in. They were sitting on the porch, enjoying the slight breeze as it brought the scent of the flowers Melanie could never get tired of admiring. She was torn between excitement being in his presence and dread that someone would happen along and interrupt them. Or worse still, that Mr. Miller would realize she had nothing of interest to say and would take his leave.

"I think she likes to be contrary." Melanie explained, "It's just a phase. While I can't say she'll ever be a seamstress, she does love being in the kitchen. And every woman ought to know her way around the animals. I wish I wasn't so squeamish myself. It would be lovely to have some chickens and a cow for fresh eggs and milk."

Cole's face was serious as he looked at her closely. "You could have those without needing to do it on your own, you know."

Melanie blinked, surprised by the sudden turn in the conversation. "Whatever do you mean? I'm afraid I barely know which end of the cow the milk comes from," she excused with a nervous giggle.

"Now I know you're teasing me, but don't you realize by now that I would love to have you out on my ranch?"

Melanie frowned at him in true confusion. "What do you mean?"

Cole sighed. "I'm not going about this at all in the right way, am I? Melanie, I know I've only known you for a few months, but in that time, I've watched you blossom from a pretty but nervous little lady to a beautiful, strong woman who would be the finest wife a rancher could hope to have. I'm proud of the progress you've made. I've grown fond of you and would deeply appreciate it if you would agree to marry me."

Melanie stared at him in shock. "That is the most lukewarm declaration I have ever heard of. I've barely seen you in the past six weeks despite the fact that your daughter has been here on three different occasions, and you expect me to believe you have suddenly developed tender feelings for me? I'm sorry to be rude, but I think you should take yourself back from wherever you came. I don't need to take on that sort of attention. I have enough of my own concerns to occupy me."

She would have giggled over the expression on his face if she weren't so very hurt by his words. Melanie had found herself pining for a visit from the handsome, rugged rancher, but knew that the depths of her own feelings required more emotion from him than what he had expressed. While it had taken her a long time to accept that she had fallen for the man, she had finally come to terms with her desire for a family of her own. And watching Katie with her doctor, Melanie knew she wouldn't settle for a weak attachment. It would need to be all or nothing for her.

Cole was still gaping at her when she turned on her heel and stormed into the house, slamming the door behind her. Melanie wished there were someone else home so she could ask them to make sure the rancher had left. She contented herself with slamming her bedroom door for good measure before throwing herself on her bed as an unexpected bout of tears claimed her.

ঋ৹ঙ

Cole sat in his wagon, pulled over to the side of the road, so as to not impede any traffic that might come along, heedless to the fact that he most likely looked like a simpleton staring off into the yonder like he was. That conversation had most certainly not gone how he had intended. Miss Jones was perfectly correct; he had stumbled through what should have been a proposal of marriage like a clumsy bull trying to drink from a teacup. All he'd done was make a mess.

But what was he going to do now? He had been so sure she returned his feelings. Maybe he had read the situation all wrong. He forced himself to pause and think back over her words. She hadn't said she didn't care for him. She just hadn't appreciated his lack of attention and the suddenness of his declaration. He couldn't really blame her for that, he supposed. It had taken him so long to figure out his own thoughts. Spending time with her had just muddled him further.

He thought of the time he had visited to help her move the flowers. She had seemed so full of light. He had the impression that he had helped her overcome some of her fears that previous day when she went to visit her customers. It had made him feel so proud of himself and of her. And then he had discussed his idea of adoption with her.

Cole loved the way she listened so attentively whenever anyone spoke to her. She had listened without interruption as he explained why he was thinking of adopting. A son to help him on his land and then to take over when he was old, seemed like a good idea.

Of course, the more time he spent with Melanie, the more he thought of a future with her. And maybe they might have more children together. Perhaps a little girl or a little boy with Melanie's bright, inquisitive eyes would fill any empty spaces still left in his heart.

The only trouble was, Cole hadn't had the best experience with women. That was why he had taken so long to come around to accepting his feelings for her. He just hoped his hesitation and blundering hadn't ruined all his chances. He would just have to convince her!

Setting his chin with determination, Cole guided his wagon to turn around slowly on the road and made short work of heading back to Melanie's tidy little house.

✤

"Melanie? Melanie!" Her name was being called, accompanied by loud banging on the door. Melanie awoke in confusion. She got to her feet and hurried to the door, sure that an emergency needed her attention.

Cole was standing there with his hat in his hand and a bemused expression on his face. It wasn't apparent what he was feeling.

"What has happened? Is Mary all right?" Melanie hadn't shaken her sleepy confusion.

Cole's eyes seemed to devour her face, and Melanie suddenly became conscious of the fact that she had fallen asleep crying. No doubt she looked a fright. She gasped as he pulled her into his arms.

"Darlin'," he drawled, "I never meant to make you cry. I'm so sorry that I saddened you with my weak expressions. I'll never make that mistake again."

Melanie's stomach began to flutter, but for the first time in her life it was a pleasurable sensation. She searched his gaze to try to read his thoughts, but he didn't leave her in suspense for long.

"While I think you will be an excellent help with Mary and a wonderful mother to any other children we might be blessed with, children don't stick around forever. I want you for me as my partner, companion, helper, and mate. I thought I could be logical about the subject. I thought I didn't need you. I'm sorry I stayed away for so long, but I was trying to get it all straight in my head."

He paused briefly, his eyes searching her gaze and examining her face, trying to gauge her reaction to his words. He ran his thumb along her cheekbone, catching the tears that had once again begun to leak from the corners of her eyes. His own eyes crinkled. "As you know, I haven't had the best of luck in the female department. My wife left me, then died, and my sister lost her mind while in my company."

Melanie made as if to protest, but he stopped her by pressing his thumb gently on her lips. "Let me finish, darlin', or I might never get this said. The thing is, I had to figure if I could deal with the responsibility of another adult in my life. I feel at enough of a loss with little Mary, but I've known her all her life, and she's mine no matter what. I've been racking my mind and heart, trying to determine if I had what it takes to make you happy. But staying away was making me miserable. I have to think that together we could manage reasonably well. We're both fine, intelligent people."

He paused again, taking a deep breath before plunging on with his speech. "I love that you are willing to face your fears. I love that your kind heart makes you speak up even when you don't want to. I love that you have taken to my daughter and helped make her feel whole, even though you didn't really want to open your heart. And I really love that you want to make Missouri home, that you won't be pining for somewhere else."

Melanie was blinking back her tears, examining his face as Cole declared himself. She felt as though her heart were going to burst, but she didn't know if she was going to be able to force words out of her mouth. It felt as though her heart were taking up all the space and preventing her thoughts from spilling out of her mouth. Finally, he grew nervous or impatient with her silence, despite what must have been obvious love shining in her eyes.

"Please, I'm begging of you, Melanie, I quite desperately love you. Please say you'll consent to be my wife, my friend, and my companion until we're both old and grey and then one of us is pushing up daisies."

Finally, Melanie gasped. "After all those beautiful words, you have to bring up our deaths?" She couldn't help but giggle a little.

"Well, that's for how long I intend to stick by your side, if you'll have me."

Melanie wound her arms around his neck and answered him simply. "I didn't think I wanted to ever marry, but I have been fighting off misery these last weeks when I haven't seen you. I thought I had given you disgust of me when I told you all about what's behind my fears and anxieties. But I appreciate that you were taking the time to be sure, I suppose. It just might've been better if you had told me what you were thinking."

"I swear to you, I will do much better in the future. Maybe if you marry me, you could teach me." His eyes were twinkling, and he wiggled his eyebrows at her.

Melanie never would have thought, if she had taken the time to imagine such a moment as this, that she would be filled with laughter at the same time as overflowing with love. But she supposed it stood to reason that happiness couldn't help but bring laughter.

"Thank you so much for your kind offer, Mr. Miller, I think I would very much like to accept."

With a shout of joy, Cole lifted her off her feet and twirled her in a circle. As he allowed her to slip back to the ground, he lowered his head and finally sealed their match with a tender kiss. As first kisses tend to do, it went slightly awry, but he quickly made up for it by wrapping his hand around the back of her head, angling her jaw slightly to the side and settling his lips more firmly over hers.

It was only when they heard a couple of loudly cleared throats that they broke apart, but not very far. Cole kept his arm wrapped tightly around Melanie's shoulder as they turned toward the gate to see who had interrupted their moment of joy and commitment.

"I knew it!" Katie declared with glee as she dashed up the stairs to hug her housemate. "I told you that you were in love with him."

Melanie couldn't help giggling in response. There was no argument to be found because it was true — she was deeply in love with the handsome rancher and couldn't wait to begin her new life by his side. All the past sorrows were forgotten as she looked deeply into her promised husband's eyes. She could see her tomorrows all laid out brightly, and a happy future beckoned her to step into it.

Epilogue

I t was a bright, warm day in September. As Melanie looked around at the gathered friends mingling about, she felt her heart swelling with gratitude and love.

Katie and Doctor Jeffries were waiting with her. Katie was standing up with her as her matron of honor as she and the doctor had just wed a couple weeks prior. Doctor Jeffries had agreed to the responsibility of walking Melanie down the aisle.

Cassandra Morley, or rather Cassie Ainsworth, and her new husband were in attendance, as well. Melanie would have never thought a socialite from New York would be attending her wedding. Not that she had ever thought she would be having a wedding, she reminded herself with a grin. But Cassie was not at all stuffy or snobby and was adjusting just as well as Melanie and Katie to her new life in Missouri.

Melanie had wondered if Cass's parents would ever accept her marriage and subsequent lack of return to New York, but the fact that they too were in attendance would seem to prove they had gotten over their anger with her for getting on the train with the orphans. It would seem there was something about Mr. Ainsworth that made them accept the situation with delight rather than the anger Melanie would have expected. She reminded herself that she needed to get the full scoop from Cassie the next time they met. Melanie had been a little too wrapped up in her own happiness to inquire as closely as she ought to into the details of Cassie's new family.

Katie and Melanie had received a letter from Sophie Brooks earlier in the week when the train stopped in town with the post. She and Renton would have loved to come for a visit, but they hadn't been able to convince Mrs. Rexford that they wanted a small wedding. It had taken Mrs. Rexford rather a long while to accept the fact that her darling son was intending to marry Sophie, but once she had, she was determined to throw the most spectacular event the city had witnessed. Melanie suppressed a shudder at the thought but was happy for her friend, who didn't seem to mind and was too caught up in her own happiness to begrudge her future mother-in-law her enjoyment.

Sophie, of course, was kind enough to want Melanie and Katie to attend her wedding along with their new husbands, but she also said she understood if they wouldn't want to return to the city so soon. Sophie promised that she and her husband would take the train out to visit them as soon as the trip could be done in less than five days. Melanie mused that with the way the train companies were pushing things, it wouldn't be long before that would be a reality.

Melanie had even received letters from both her sister and her brother. Her sister had baby number two on the way, so she wasn't up to the trip West but sent her love and best wishes, which meant so much to the big sister. Even Henry had something kind to say, much to Melanie's surprise, and sent a little money as a wedding gift, which she never would have expected, since he had been the most miserly boy she had ever seen as soon as he received his inheritance. Perhaps they would be able to maintain a relationship through the post.

Finally, it was time. Katie finished fussing with Melanie's hem; there was nothing more that could be done to the beautiful gown. It was the most wonderful garment the two women had made, in Melanie's doting opinion. It had been crafted with love and joy so nothing more could be expected of it. Melanie couldn't help but feel beautiful as she took one last glance at herself to make sure her hair was staying in place.

Mary and Annie danced into the room in a whirl of energy and swinging pink taffeta.

"You look beautiful," Mary breathed in awe.

Melanie laughed. "That is sweet of you to say. The two of you look to be glowing. Are you ready?"

Both girls nodded vigorously, thrilled to be a part of the special day. Melanie thought back on the moment when she and Cole had told Mary that they were to wed. The little girl had been beside herself with joy. Her only disappointment was that Annie wasn't going to be joining their household as well. They assured her they were still considering sending to Mrs. Parker for at least one orphan of their own.

"Then let's go," Melanie declared, sharing a grin with Katie as the two girls made to dash from the room.

"Try for some decorum," Katie called after them, and their strides shortened minutely. "I better try to keep up with them, but don't you rush — you need to savor the moment." Katie looked stern before her expression turned sly. "And you need to make your groom savor the moment, too."

Melanie's face heated in a blush, which was probably Katie's intention. She had always been such a teasing friend. Melanie couldn't believe that both of them were getting a happily ever after.

By then, she and Doctor Jeffries were joining the rest, and Melanie's gaze had been ensnared by Cole's. All other thoughts slipped away on the breeze. All she could think about was her love for this man and the joy with which she was facing her future. She knew the minister was saying some beautiful words that she ought to be pondering, but she couldn't bring herself to pay attention. Before she knew it, she was stammering after him, making her vows, and then it was official. She was Mrs. Cole Miller. The gathered townsfolk cheered and clapped as Cole bent his head and captured her breath and her lips with his warm embrace.

The End

Enjoyed this and the previous stories?
Consider the *Boxed Set* containing all four books of the

Orphan Train Series

Read about three young women as they accompany a train load of orphans traveling to their new lives out West. The women find love while helping the children find happiness.

Enjoy this four-book series written exclusively by Wendy May Andrews.

Stay in touch with Wendy May Andrews
and forthcoming publishing news.

Sign up for her biweekly newsletter

About the Author

I've been writing pretty much since I learned to read when I was five years old. Of course, those early efforts were basically only something a mother could love ☺ I put writing aside after I left school and stuck with reading. I am an avid reader. I love words. I will read anything, even the cereal box, signs, posters, etc. But my true love is novels.

Almost ten years ago my husband dared me to write a book instead of always reading them. I didn't think I'd be able to do it, but to my surprise I love writing. Those early efforts eventually became my first published book – *Tempting the Earl* (published by Avalon books in 2010). There were some ups and downs in my publishing efforts. My first publisher was sold and I became an "orphan" author, back to the drawing board of trying to find a publishing house. It has been a thrilling adventure as I learned to navigate the world of publishing.

I believe firmly that everyone deserves a happily ever after. I want my readers to be able to escape from the everyday for a little while and feel upbeat and refreshed when they get to the end of my books.

When not reading or writing, I can be found traipsing around my neighborhood admiring the dogs and greenery or travelling the world with my favorite companion.

Stay in touch:

Website Facebook Instagram Twitter

www.ingramcontent.com/pod-product-compliance
Lightning Source LLC
Chambersburg PA
CBHW061221210726
48294CB00006B/1923